Zoo

The Cheshire Prize for Literature Anthologies

Prize Flights: Stories from the Cheshire Prize for Literature 2003; edited by Ashley Chantler

Life Lines: Poems from the Cheshire Prize for Literature 2004; edited by Ashley Chantler

Word Weaving: Stories and Poems for Children from the Cheshire Prize for Literature 2005; edited by Jaki Brien

Edge Words: Stories from the Cheshire Prize for Literature 2006; edited by Peter Blair

Elements: Poems from the Cheshire Prize for Literature 2007; edited by Peter Blair

Wordscapes: Stories and Poems for Children from the Cheshire Prize for Literature 2008; edited by Jaki Brien

Zoo

Short Stories from the Cheshire Prize for Literature 2009

Edited by Emma Rees

Chester Academic Press

First Published 2010
by Chester Academic Press
University of Chester
Parkgate Road
Chester CH1 4BJ

Printed and bound in the UK by the
LIS Print Unit
University of Chester
Cover designed by the
LIS Graphics Team
University of Chester

A catalogue record of this book is available
from the British Library

ISBN 978-1-905929-83-2

CONTENTS

THE CONTRIBUTORS

Annette Albuquerque was born and brought up in Chester. She graduated from Manchester University (long ago) and embarked on a series of casual jobs before settling into a teaching career. For several happy years, she taught at a fabulously unconventional prep school in Central London which became the setting for her story for *Zoo*, "The Sitting Tenant." As far as she knows, the real school has not suffered the same fate. These days, she is largely defined by her role as wife and mother, although she still works as a supply teacher in Wirral. Time off for good behaviour is spent writing, painting and running the occasional children's drama course.

Jan Bengree is a Cestrian. She has taught in London and Cheshire, and currently tutors WEA Creative Writers locally. Her stories and articles have been published in magazines and anthologies, including the University of Chester's *Flash* magazine, and also broadcast on radio. She has won several writing prizes and been shortlisted in various competitions. Jan is a member of Chester Writers and she instigated its spin-off group, "Words and Biscuits." She lives with her husband and tabby cats, and has a grown-up family, plus three grandchildren.

Madeleine Beveridge grew up in Middlewich and has very pleasant memories of canals, salt, and entire summer holidays spent in the town's small library. She recently returned from three years working in Japan, and is experiencing strong withdrawal symptoms for anthropomorphic seaweed snacks. She is now a postgraduate student at the University of Edinburgh. She studies how people's eyes move as they read text. Her long-term ambition is to emulate Miss Marple and spend her retirement solving gruesome murders from her picturesque country cottage.

Die Booth lives in Chester with the ghosts and likes cats, playing fiddle, and exploring abandoned buildings. Past occupations include making dolls' shoes, singing harmonies in a horror punk band and framing pictures. Die is currently working on a second novel and has had numerous short stories published in anthologies and magazines. This is the second story from Die that has featured in a Cheshire Prize for Literature Anthology. You can say hi at: http://diebooth.wordpress.com/

Oliver Briscoe is 34 and is originally from Norfolk. He moved to Chester from Norwich, although he denies he only lives in cities with walls. He has had a varied career in journalism and PR, including local newspapers, national magazines and also working in marketing museums. He is currently working for a local housing association. Like all journalists, he has always wanted to write something more creative and occasionally he manages it. His interests include history, cycling and Belgian beer and his literary heroes include Jane Austen and Neil Gaiman.

Rachael Bundock was born in Southport in 1990, and has lived all over England (and in America for a brief period). She is currently studying English with Creative Writing at the University of Chester. When she's not at university, she lives in Surrey with her father and brother. She has been writing since she was 13, and has had poetry published in the University's creative writing magazine, as well as an article in the University newspaper. She loves foreign languages and hopes to travel around Europe and Asia after graduating (to postpone starting work for as long as possible!).

Sophie Coulombeau was born in London in 1984, but grew up in Cheshire. After taking an undergraduate degree in English Literature, she went on to travel in Europe, Canada and South America, and did postgraduate work at the University of Pennsylvania under a Thouron Fellowship. She currently lives in Brussels, fighting organized crime by day and scribbling by night. She is working on a collection of short stories and a novel, and is very grateful to the editor of *Zoo* for publishing "High Flyer" and thereby giving her the confidence to forge ahead with bigger and scarier projects.

Helen Dalton is 22 years old and this is the first short story competition that she has entered. She attended Stockport Grammar School in Cheshire but currently lives in Derbyshire. She recently completed her undergraduate degree in Classics at Durham and will be reading for an MPhil at Cambridge from October 2010. She is an avid reader and also enjoys playing the saxophone in her spare time.

David Diggory was born in Manchester but moved to Cheshire when he was three years old. He's been here ever since, apart from time spent as a lawyer in London and Norway. It was in Norway he had the penguin idea. Penguins were wandering down the Oslo streets. That's what he told his niece, aged eight, at the time. Then, working as an English Language teacher, he had the notion of a student stealing one. Now he's seeing penguins everywhere!

Max Dunbar was born in London in 1981, and now lives in Manchester. He recently finished a full-length novel and his short fiction has appeared in various print and web journals including *Open Wide, Straight from the Fridge* and *Lamport Court.* He also writes criticism for *3:AM* and *Butterflies and Wheels.* He is Manchester's regional editor of *Succour* magazine, a journal of new fiction and poetry. He blogs at: http://maxdunbar.wordpress.com/

Heather Freckleton's mother was a brilliant story teller and her example encouraged Heather to begin writing from an early age. Through the years her writing has been sporadic and it's only fairly recently that she's been able to give it a more powerful focus. She's had some small success with poetry and, now, with this short story. She's met people from many different backgrounds through travel, working in social work and living in many places. These experiences have given her a rich well to draw from. She was brought up in Birmingham and has lived in Chester for the past 10 years.

Simon Gotts has recently moved to Wales, having lived in Chester for nearly two decades. He is still a member of Chester Writers, among whom he has made many good friends over the years. In his stories he likes to illustrate character by showing ordinary people at times of minor crisis, believing that devastatingly violent events are not the stuff of most people's experience. He won the Cheshire Prize short story competition in 2006.

Gillian Higgs was born and educated in Leeds, and then studied English and Latin at the University of Liverpool. She worked for a short time as a teacher, married a psychiatrist, and lived in Bermuda, Birmingham and Manchester before settling with their two daughters on a smallholding in Cheshire in 1985. She has recently completed a diploma in garden design at Reaseheath College, and is interested in sustainable use of the land for both gardening and agriculture. Bird watching, walking, reading and cooking occupy her when she is not looking after the hens, cows and sheep.

Sarah Hilary is an award-winning writer and reviewer whose fiction appears in *The Fish Anthology, Smokelong Quarterly, The Best of Every Day Fiction*, and in the Crime Writers' Association anthology, *MO: Crimes of Practice*. Sarah won the Fish Historical Crime Prize in 2008, and was a finalist in the Biscuit Contest. Most recently, her work was Highly Commended by *Aesthetica* and nominated for the Pushcart Prize. A non-fiction column about the wartime experiences of her mother, who was a child internee of the Japanese, was published in *Foto8 Magazine* and later in the *Bristol Review of Books*. Sarah blogs at: http://sarah-crawl-space.blogspot.com/

Emily-Jo Hopson is 21 and lives in the middle of a field on the Welsh border with her mother, an artist. She is currently studying Creative Writing with History at the University of Chester, and hopes to pursue an MA after graduating. Her career began fifteen years ago with a half-page text on evolution, written in green felt tip. Nowadays, Emily writes fiction. Her influences include Roald Dahl, Nicole Krauss, Angela Carter, Luke Sutherland and Jeffrey Eugenides.

Richard Lakin started writing to escape some of the routine horrors of police work. He still writes to escape work, but also to entertain himself and hopefully others. He writes to learn about people and landscapes and to find a quiet place to think on a crowded commuter train. He's worked as a police officer, a sales rep and a journalist. Listening and watching people is part of the fascination. There are stories all around us, but greasy spoon cafés and coffee shops are his preferred outlets. He's married with two young sons who are already making up their own stories.

John Latham was born and grew up in Frodsham, Cheshire. He is an atmospheric scientist, formerly Head of the Physics Department, Manchester University, now Senior Research Fellow at the National Centre for Atmospheric Research, Boulder, Colorado. His research is on lightning and on a "cloud whitening" idea he published in *Nature* (1990) for producing controlled global cooling to balance global warming. In 2008 the new atmospheric research laboratories at Manchester University were named after him. He is also a writer, having published five volumes of poetry and a novel. He has won first prize in about 25 UK national poetry competitions, and has had three plays and numerous stories broadcast on BBC national radio. Much of his writing, from a child's perspective, is located in war-time Frodsham, particularly on the Hill, from where he and his friends on stormy days could see Germany – and Hitler.

Alison Leonard has written fiction for children and young adults, and drama for BBC radio. She is married with two adult daughters, and recently graduated from Manchester Metropolitan University with an MA in Creative Writing (with distinction). The story included in *Zoo* arose from her research for a novel called *Flesh and Bronze*, which brings to life a woman who modelled for the artist Degas.

Catherine Marseille is originally from Munich, Germany where she practised dance and theatre in her free time and taught herself Japanese. Before she started studying in Chester, she lived and worked in Tokyo for over a year. In 2009 she graduated with a degree in English Literature with German from the University of Chester and is currently looking into doing a PhD. She is one of the founding editors of *Albatross*, a poetry magazine edited by students in Chester, and enjoys Chester's open mic poetry nights on a regular basis. She is also a freelance Manga artist.

Sheila Powell is a teacher, walker, reader and gardener and has been writing for years. She has had some success in competitions but her primary ambition is to see one of her children's stories illustrated and published. She is generally inspired by nature, magic and time although this story in *Zoo* is something of a deviation and was actually inspired by a dead sheep and a washing line full of teddy bears and baby clothes – which only goes to show that inspiration can come from anywhere.

Emma Rees (Editor, and Chair, Judging Panel) is Deputy Head of English and Senior Lecturer at the University of Chester. Her *Margaret Cavendish* was published in 2004, and she is currently working on *Can't: Uncovering the Postmodern Vagina*. She has contributed essays to recent books including one on Shakespeare and gender for *Rhetorics of Bodily Disease and Health in Medieval and Early Modern England*; one on 19th-century gynaecology for *The Female Body in Medicine and Literature*; a section on Shakespeare and the Renaissance for *Studying Literature*; and a chapter, co-authored with Richard E. Wilson, on Freudian fetishism, in *Led Zeppelin and Philosophy*. Emma was born and bred in Birmingham, moving to Chester in 1999 after living in Norwich for several years, where she taught at UEA. She spends what little spare time she has with her husband, teenage daughter, five cats and dog, at home in Handbridge. She spends what little spare cash she has on going to rock concerts; on buying books and stationery; and on running a tremendously impractical but beautiful car.

Tessa Sheridan, a filmmaker and screenwriter, has long nursed a disloyal addiction to short stories. She believes them to be the finest things contemporary fiction has to offer, and the hardest nuts to crack. Reading turned to writing, as these things do, and the rest is mostly ink stains, waste bins and the crying bit in between. A few sorry nuggets survive. Her story in *Zoo*, "That Going to the Zoo Thing," is one of a series of tales voiced by characters whose internal logic is irreproachably consistent yet sadly flawed. The best that can be said about these people is that they nurse a suspicion, as does the writer herself, that they may just have got the wrong end of the stick about everything.

Lynne Voyce grew up in Ellesmere Port and completed her 'A'-levels at what used to be Chester College of Further Education. She now lives in Birmingham with her husband and two daughters, where she teaches English in an inner city comprehensive school. Her work has appeared in *Raw*

Edge, Libbon, Strandline, Wordsmag and the anthologies *The Better Craftsman and Other Stories; The Light that Remains and Other Stories* (both Leaf Books); and *With Islands in Mind* (Earlyworks Press). She has won the Legend Writing Award, the Ted Walters International Short Story Competition, and has been placed in numerous other competitions. Her works have been performed in venues across the North and the West Midlands. In 2007 she was given an Arts Council of England Creative Ambition Award. She fits writing around employment, family and an unhealthy obsession with celebrity gossip.

Kaite Welsh is an author, activist and freelance journalist. She is finishing her first novel, an historical fantasy for teenagers set in Victorian Wales, called *A Tyrant Spell*. She lives in London with her partner and cats, and refuses to accept that she has too many books. She blogs sporadically on her website: www.kaitewelsh.posterous.com/

FOREWORD

> I'm a failed poet. Maybe every novelist wants to write poetry first, finds he can't, and then tries the short story which is the most demanding form after poetry. And failing at that, only then does he take up novel writing.

The Nobel Laureate William Faulkner was being ironic, of course, in declaring this, but he was also suggesting something important about how very difficult it is to write a good short story where form and content must work in perfect symbiosis. A successful short story shines like a jewel: entire and dazzling, refracting the reader's thoughts through the prism of its perfection. The weaker entries for the 2009 High Sheriff's Cheshire Prize for Literature did not display an understanding of the subtleties of the form – they read, rather, like extracts or chapters from novels or, worse, like the publisher's blurb from a back cover. By contrast, the stronger entries displayed a deft handling of the paradoxically limiting *and* liberating potential of the medium.

The stories which make up this anthology not only control the form, but they also find and maintain consistent and authentic narrative voices. Once the writer has found and established those voices we, as readers, are allowed temporarily and absolutely to inhabit a new perspective, from which we emerge, inevitably, changed. So it is that in this collection we experience the anxiety of social misfits; encounter darkness, isolation, and cruelty; smile in recognition of our own eccentricities; and grieve at the irremediable nature of loss.

The overall winner of the 2009 Prize was Tessa Sheridan for "That Going to the Zoo Thing." Simon Gotts was the runner-up for his story "Summer Show: Schedule of Events;" Die Booth and Heather Freckleton were highly commended for their stories. Tessa's story suggested the title for this collection, but *Zoo* seemed apt for other reasons, too. The nature of an anthology is that the reader can meander past some stories, reading others first, just as the visitor to a zoo can head straight for the snow leopards, leaving the meerkats and bats until the walk back to the car park. Similarly, at the zoo, we may be delighted by exotic creatures or marvel at the mundane, noticing things we'd never really considered before - so it is with the stories in this collection. The zoo is also a classless, ageless place: as with this anthology, there is in it something to please everyone. Each story demands that we engage with it and, for the space of a few pages at least, connect absolutely with life as mediated through the lens of another's experience.

I would like to thank my colleagues on the judging panel: John Scrivener and Francesca Haig. I would also like to thank the writer Tim Firth who did such a splendid job of reading the winning entries at the prize-giving evening, where the High Sheriff of Cheshire, William Ferguson, announced the names of the winners. Lynda Baguley and Jenni Westcott have been wonderful organisers and administrators throughout the competition, from its inception, to the publication of this anthology. I am also tremendously grateful for the help of Graham Atkin, Peter Blair, Ashley Chantler, Melissa Fegan, Sarah Heaton, Yvonne

Siddle, Alan Wall and Richard E. Wilson. Thanks are also due to Bank of America for their sterling support of the competition.

Emma Rees
Chair, Judging Panel, and Editor, *Zoo*
Department of English
University of Chester
31 March 2010

THAT GOING TO THE ZOO THING

Tessa Sheridan

That going to the zoo thing can go one of two ways, depending. With Gerard it went like this:

He doesn't ring for nineteen days and five hours. Then he rings and says *we need to* and I say *yes, we need to do something about our relationship*, which is a line I read in a magazine at the doctor's. But he's been talking at the same time and after a few seconds I hear it like an echo and what he's said is, let's go to the zoo.

So I'm thinking this is a long way of doing a short thing. I'm poking at my cuticles trying to get the fishy smell out and I'm wondering how it's going to be. We'll be strolling past the chimps and he'll go: sometimes I think we're like chimps, you and me, we look like we're smiling but we're just not.

Or he'll stop by the antelope enclosure and sigh a bit and say: I look at them, Jude, and they all look the same, but really when you think about it you're an antelope and I've always been 99% ibex, simple as that.

It'd be hard to consider the antelope and the ibex and not agree with him. Me with my orange roots where the dye didn't work; him with his tortoiseshell glasses and his childbearing hips.

But when you've finally got a boyfriend the important thing is to stop him going away and being someone else's boyfriend. I'm not exactly sure why because that was in part two of the magazine, which was when the doctor called me in.

It's a shame in a way because lately Gerard had made me want to make that sound the cat makes when something's got stuck in its throat. It's a nice sound, don't get me wrong. But you wouldn't want to make it forever.

Still, I did what the magazine said and listed the positives. There were two, which is what the experts call a shortlist.

> One: he was a boyfriend.
> Two: we shared hobbies.

Gerard's hobby was thinking, which is a good hobby. He shared it with me a lot. Although he did it quietly so that's just a guess. His favourite thinker was Sartre, who is dead and thought mostly in French. I shared my hobby too, which was talking. Gerard was someone I could talk to. Or at least I talked when I was standing next to him, which is nearly the same thing. I said to him, we're a good match, you with your thoughts and me with my words. Together we can make sentences.

Gerard said I had to make up my own thoughts. Looking back, maybe that's where the rot set in.

I'm not cut out for a life of the mind. When I left school I wanted to be a caterer. Not in the conventional sense. I meant more catering as an idea. The idea that appealed best was catering to the needs of monks. These could be any kind of needs, I'm not prejudiced, and they wouldn't exclude sexual needs. The monk would have the need and my job would be to make the need go away so I could stay on the island and watch the puffins. That was how I saw it in my mind. But the careers lady said perhaps the fish factory was a way to start, to get on the career ladder was how she put it. Then she smiled and said *progress, not perfection,* which was nice. Anyway I couldn't disagree because I was trying to remember the words so I could use them in a little thought to try out on Gerard.

I met him where you're supposed to meet boys, at a bus stop. I'd been going there for months ever since I'd found out that was the right place. I went after my shift and stayed until the last bus went. He got off the C56 one night while I was away in the bushes taking a pee and I had to run to catch him up. It was pretty dark and I made a little grab at him as he crossed the road and next thing he's holding out his wallet and screaming: *take it take it don't touch my glasses!*

I knew right away that's the kind of story the best man tells at the reception. How they met, Jude and Gerard. There'd be a line at the end I hadn't worked out yet, something like: *and she's been jumping on him ever since!*

That's the way it was supposed to go. But it must've gone another way because here we were going to Chester Zoo to do the breaking up thing.

Even so, I was getting pretty excited. I'd never actually been to a zoo. Mother said she was allergic to them; that's why we had to go to church instead. Come Saturday I'm lining up jokes connected with animals in case they come in handy. There's the cheetah/cheater joke and the constipated elephant one, which Gerard had to explain to me the first time. It seemed unlikely he'd want to hear the same joke twice but you never know. I'm counting up the positives as I've already said. Another thing I'm doing is skipping up and down the landing. I do this to wear myself out so I don't do silly immature things that are beneath me, like that business with the revolving doors which I won't go into now.

So then I'm ready.

As I said before, it can go one of two ways at this point. In Version One Gerard doesn't turn up. Dumping me outside the zoo would be like a kind of code. One of his little thoughts. In that version I'd wait all day then I'd go home to bed and stay there for months trying to crack the code, and end up in a mental home going *la la la* to the wallpaper.

But Version Two is what happened. In this version he met me inside and we walked about a bit. Then he sat in the picnic area near the snake house and cried. I didn't know what to do so I ate my Jaffa Cakes. He said he felt alone and unloved in the world. The universe was a limitless place and yet he felt constricted and misunderstood. I could feel a thought coming on. *Like a snake!* I said, maybe a bit too loud. *Like a snake in – in a fish bowl! Like, the snake's in totally the wrong place but nobody gets it!* I had to laugh, I was so happy I'd thought it up. But Gerard just looked at me through the tortoiseshell glasses and after a bit he shook his head like I was something stuck to his eyelash. Then he carried on staring at the sweet wrappers in the grass. After a bit I got cold so I left him there.

On the bus back I found a bunch of straw in my pocket. I'd picked it up in the pig pen meaning to feed it to the hippos if we ever got that far. We never did.

I keep it in my purse, just in case.

Gerard said hell is other people. Sartre said it first, to be fair. He said it in French when he was alive of course. But he never said which people exactly.

I'm not the type to jump to conclusions. But I've been practising this thinking thing and what I'm thinking is this:

I think it might be me.

SUMMER SHOW: SCHEDULE OF EVENTS

Simon Gotts

1.00 pm: Young Stock In Hand: Rare or Minority Breed

Seeing Ann Griffiths's hair plastered to her head Beryl thinks of the grass in the fields, beaten limp by the sun, ground under hundreds of car tyres and boot heels. The grass will recover after a shower, but Mrs Griffiths's hair will need costly attention from Glen at the Last Chance Salon.

"Be a love, Beryl and split that load of baps. I'll see if I can magic up some more tuna."

The bag is keeping cool in the patch of clover by the door flap, but the polythene shows rivulets of condensation as though someone has breathed into it. Beryl sticks her head experimentally out into the air and the sun is fiercer than ever. She returns to the swampy atmosphere of the tent.

"Come and help me with these baps, Macey. I'll split, you butter. See if I can keep up with you."

Macey is a perfectionist. Every millimetre must be evenly covered. She slips her tongue back in her mouth when Beryl catches her eye.

"Where's Luke?"

"Luke's helping serve dinners."

Macey looks round the trestle tables and sees him standing next to Mrs Maskell, handing out plates and cutlery.

"I want to serve dinners."

"Well, these are dinners. They're dinners you can take away if you're too busy to sit down. A lot of the judges don't sit down all day."

"I want to sit down."

"Let's finish these baps first."

Macey shrugs and resumes her buttering. Beryl watches her warily. According to Mrs Maskell Macey is apt to get nose bleeds when she's stressed. She finishes one bap and slumps onto a canvas chair. An old gent in a tan suit and white overcoat sidles to their table. He wears a red ribbon on his lapel with "Poultry" printed in yellow. One eye twinkles, the other is cloudy, like an egg on the turn. He rubs his face with a large, linen hankie, till it is blotchy pink.

"Would you like to pour this gentleman some lemonade, Macey?"

You could walk past her in the street and never know, according to Mrs Maskell. She pours the drink obediently, unsmiling, concentrating on filling the cup right to the brim. The judge twinkles with his good eye, but when she has finished her task Macey shivers and turns away.

"Can I go round the stalls now?"

Beryl glances towards Mrs Griffiths, who is busy helping Luke keep the ham he is serving from slicking off the judges' plates onto the grass.

"Well, take care. Go round once and come straight back." She unzips her money belt. "Get yourself an ice lolly."

"Mrs Griffiths gave me some money."

Beryl hands her the heavy-duty carrier bag with which she travels. Macey turns and closes in on herself. She walks through the crowds round-shouldered, like a dusk-dwelling beetle caught in the glare of midday.

"Dad's been made redundant," Mrs Maskell confides. "Big brother's in Afghanistan."

***

1.40 pm: Judging of Sheep and Goats

Beryl and Sally Maskell are having five minutes while Ann ropes in her husband and grown-up daughter to serve puddings.

"It was coincidence," Beryl says. "Ann was in the chair next to me at the Last Chance Salon and she noticed how thin my hair was. We got talking and I said I'd sort of promised that if I got well again I'd stop working for Idris at the partnership and do something that made a *difference*. She said she'd done the same sort of thing ten years ago and started up this little charity group."

"Who did you promise?"

"Who? Well I never really said it out loud."

Mrs Maskell leans over the iced fancies on the paper napkin they are sharing. "Did you promise God?"

"It's hard to remember. You get this sort of chemo-fog."

"Do you like these with the crystallized orange? I'll have it then, shall I?"

"When I was over the worst, physically, I went into a depression."

"I think Ann's overdone the eking out. This lemonade's gone back to water."

"I'd been taking it one day at a time for so long, when I realised I might have a future I didn't want to face it. I thought, I've been saved, but I don't know what for."

"Did you ask God about it? I ask him about all sorts – should I buy the *Big Issue*? Should I travel by train to save greenhouse gas?"

"To be honest, Sally, God pretty much kept his head down. Idris was the one who told me to stop worrying about the future and volunteer for something - put all the angst to one side. Actually, what he said was, "Shove it all on the Shit Shelf, Bee"."

If Idris were here he would say that Mrs Maskell's face looks like a smacked arse.

A small red spot on the paper napkin catches Beryl's eye. Another, in her cup of milk and another on the fancy with white icing and silver balls. The spots burst like tiny speeded-up flowers. Beryl turns and Macey is standing over her shoulder with a dripping tissue clamped to her nose.

"I've lost my purse."

Having established that Macey's purse is bright, shiny pink and contains her money, her bus pass, her library card and her inhaler Mrs Griffiths organizes a search. Sally Maskell will scour the stalls, while Mr Griffiths takes in the show rings and his daughter the rides and marquees. Mrs Griffiths is too exhausted to search, but instructs Luke to go round the tent, which he does on all fours, snuffling like a bloodhound. Macey is told to go and sit in a corner and pinch her nose.

The last ice dwindles in the cool box. Beryl scrapes leftovers into black sacks. The judges are out on their rounds and only the bluebottles are interested in the food. Ann Griffiths eases onto a chair, fanning herself with a programme.

"Every year I say this is my last fundraiser." She blows out her purple cheeks. "By the way, what's happened to Macey?"

***

2.20 pm: VIP Tour of Showground

"Means, Motive, Opportunity – the three Ms. Except that's two Ms and an O, so it must be Means, Motive, Method or Means Motive, Monsters or Milk, Marmalade, Masturbation. Have you seen *CSI*? *Prime Suspect*? *Wire in the Blood*? When somebody's murdered they can tell how long they've been dead by taking the maggots out and seeing what stage they're at –"

"Macey hasn't been murdered, Luke. She's just got lost. We'll find her quicker if you talk less and look harder. She's probably searching for her purse. It's got all her important things in."

There is no sign of Macey at the stalls, so Beryl tries the portable loos. She walks along the row knocking on each of the ten doors, calling Macey's name.

"These are like the Tardis. She could've been taken to the future. Or there might have been a man hiding in there with a knife, or she could've had an attack and choked on her own vomit. You only have to inhale about three grams."

Beryl strides past the sheep pens leaving Luke trailing. A row of box-faced Texels follow her with their sceptical eyes. Past the sleeping bulls, heavy horses and vintage machinery, one deep breath through poultry and on round produce with ruthless use of the elbows. She reaches the main ring, where the Factor-Ex Stunt Bikers are repeatedly jumping two of the three transit vans they arrived in. The crowd is listless and unresponsive, slouched on straw bales in the dizzying sun.

Beryl throws up her arms and moans, "Why? Why am I doing this?"

Luke digs in his jeans and brings out the purse.

"I didn't bloody steal it. I found it in a carrier bag. You shouldn't use plastic bags, anyway – they're bad for the environment."

***

6.00 pm: Parade of Show Queen

Idris has the top down on the BMW. He raises an eyebrow, but gives Macey a smile.

"I promised Macey we'd give her a ride home in a sports car."

"Fine. How'd it go, today?"

"Pretty well. Insofar as nobody died, did they Macey?"

Idris gets out to let Macey into the back seat. He takes a longer look and decides to strap her in himself.

"I've upset Sally Maskell, Mrs Griffiths collapsed from heat stroke, Macey got lost, and the young policeman who found her asleep in the bikers' spare van put his hand on a wasp."

He pulls out behind the last of the horse-boxes, laughing. In a few minutes they turn out of the gate and are speeding down cool, green lanes.

Beryl turns in her seat. Macey has her nose in the air, eyes half closed, her hair flaming out behind her like an orange flag. She moves her head from side to side catching the wind in her smile. She is beautiful.

THE AUDSLEY CHIMERA

Die Booth

"Dad, when did unicorns go extinct?"

I remember asking that question. Dad said, "They're not extinct, they're a made-up animal."

"Like seahorses?" I asked. Dad laughed.

"Seahorses are real, you daft-head, you know that."

"Oh yeah."

I thought about seahorses. I thought about seahorses a lot. My version was man-sized and foaming white as wave-crests, dragging people out to sea. The mild, invisible-coloured wafers that sank sadly in aquarium tanks seemed an unlikely substitute to me.

"Are pegasuses real too, then?" Really, I knew the answer, I just wasn't sure of its authenticity.

"You've been watching too many films," said Dad.

"But they could be real. You could get a horse to have babies with an eagle ..."

"It doesn't work like that, Nicky."

An owl? A swan? I tried to think of a bird big enough. "Why can't you just sew some wings on a horse, then?"

Dad insisted it wouldn't work. He couldn't quite say why, just that it would be a bad idea. I suppose he couldn't think of a way to explain tissue rejection and ethics to a nine-year-old. Or maybe he just knew that it must possible and he didn't know how to deny it.

Dad was always trying to protect me from reality.

"Come home by the main road, Nicky." *Don't go into the Wedge on your own.* The Wedge was an anachronism of woodland that embarrassed suburbia for two miles in the middle of our Audsley housing estate. Ancient woodland, other-worldly and rare: they said it harboured vermin, and perverts.

Dad said children shouldn't go off with strange men, because the men would do things to them. Like his ambiguity about the realisation of dreams, Dad couldn't elaborate on what these things were. "Bad things," he'd say. Bad, like growing wings on horses. Mysterious things, I thought, *exciting*.

***

This boy is too young to walk in the woods alone.

He's a small child, his fingers delicate as feather shafts, swinging an ash branch from side to side as he trudges without purpose. The stick scythes through foxgloves, disturbing something and the boy freezes. When he hears the kitten's cry he relaxes. Parting the ferns, confusion, fear and delight carousel across his face.

***

When I was little I loved the zoo.

The zoo had its own rail stop, with smiling cartoon animals coexisting peaceably on the pocked metal sign. Eventually the staff at the ticket office got to know me by name and I didn't even have to ask for Aunty Gill to gain my free entry.

The faux-jungle floor was littered with the rainbow of my crayons. I sat cross-legged, matching halves in my sketchbook: the beasts on my pages had eagle wings and the tails of snakes. Pacing behind the glass, the spotted cats spoke to me with lantern eyes.

"Let me out of here," they said, "Let me fly."

***

There's a hiss of grass as the branch falls from the boy's hand.

The kitten totters, mewing angrily: a tabby with yellow eyes and, arcing improbably from its tiny shoulder blades, a pair of tawny wings. The boy: stunned into silence. The kitten spreads its wings, the flight feathers fanning, but it's too weak yet to flap.

I'm working on that one.

***

I started with insects. I spliced them together using the craft blades from my modelling kit: if all children pull the wings off flies, then pulling the wings off flies and grafting them onto caterpillars is no worse.

They died, of course.

Maybe I would've given up if it wasn't for seeing a sign. I was at the end of the garden path, in the part where grown-ups didn't go. Behind the unruly barricade of pampas grass that unzipped red crosshatches on your skin, where a stack of old bikes rusted comfortably against the shed door, I lay on my stomach on the warm flagstones and watched a worm take its weight onto new spider legs and stand. Those few seconds before it curled and died, I knew my calling: not to destroy, but to transform.

***

He picks it up, of course, cradles the kitten to his chest and looks around for someone to show. There is nobody. Wading through the bracken, foliage as high as his waistband leaves rainwater swipes across his tracksuit. When he reaches the clearing he stops, blandly assessing the scenario: a little house with nets in the windows. Who would live in the woods? But children don't read fairytales anymore. I let the nets fall back into place and go to open the door.

He doesn't sound too cautious, but I can tell he's not stupid.

"Is this your cat, mister?"

I lean against the doorframe and smile.

"Let me see; that depends if he has wings or not." The boy proudly holds the kitten up. It wriggles, outraged, in his grip. "Icarus! You found him. I've been looking all over the place for him."

"What's he called?" asks the boy suspiciously. I open the door wider, so he can see the cages inside.

"Icarus. Like the Greek myth."

"What's a myth?"

What's a myth. We are our own gods; we will be legend.

I say, "It's a type of story. Thank you for finding him."

Icarus's claws snag in the fabric of the boy's shirt as he reluctantly hands him over. I shake my head.

"It looks like he's quite attached to you. Would you like to meet his brothers and sisters?"

"You got more of them?"

I nod. "Oh, yes."

"Have they got wings?"

"Some of them."

The boy peers past me at the wall of cages, at the jewel-hued feathers and striped fur. Hugging the winged kitten, he steps through the door.

"What's your name, son?"

"Michael." His eyes brighten at "son." Perhaps he never was one before.

"Hello, Michael. I'm Nick."

"Hi."

Learning my name has prompted his first shyness. Still, Michael gazes into the cages with undisguised delight and I watch over his shoulder as the parrot asks him for a biscuit, holding out its paws imploringly.

I will not call them experiments.

In the beginning, I picked them up from rescue centres. Last-chancers with no future - I saved them from the needle with the knife. I was a pioneer. They found me out when I was seventeen and I was sent to a psychiatrist. It didn't end happily; I had to run. My first success was what it took, a dog I named Trojan; a bull mongrel with horns. I sold him to a drug baron and my reputation was made. Now my research is funded by eccentrics and magnates and society remains oblivious. It's easy to become invisible if you have money. They get their exotic pets; I get my anonymity. Wings are my favourite. I swap and change, improving nature, recreating legend. I want a gryphon. I want so much more. Perhaps the greatest medical talent of two centuries: I can say that without bragging but I have to hide. Beneath the trees, the bones of failed operations soften in the dirt.

Michael stops in front of the last cage.

"What's that?"

"A swan."

"A magic swan?" His tone is that of a child too entrenched in reality to dare to hope.

"No, just a normal swan."

The boy looks resigned. "The Queen owns all the swans" he says. I'm charmed.

"Now, how do you know that?"

"I seen it on telly." He looks around, openly. "Can I feed the bird cat?"

"You certainly may."

"Can I have something, too?"

"What would you like?"

He looks at me like it's his birthday. Really, it is.

"Chocolate," he says.

The cocoa I find in the cupboard is months out of date, but I doubt that the boy will object. The milk is creamy and thickens in the pan.

I mix it sweet to hide any bitterness.

The boy blows on his mug to cool it while he drinks. Immediately, he yawns.

"Are you tired, Michael?"

"No," he insists.

I say, "I think the bird cat is tired. Will you lie down on the settee with him so he can get some sleep?"

Michael nods silently, dragging his knuckles across his eyes. I can imagine what he's seeing now: little threads of light crawling across his vision like a virus under a microscope; he shakes his head to clear it and the room tips and spins. I plump the cushions. His eyes are already closed. His hair is a feather fan of almost-white.

I look towards my animals, my fantastic zoo that nature cannot rival. I look at the caged swan, its wings spanning the width of the enclosure as it stretches. I look at the perfect boy asleep on the settee, the winged kitten curled on his belly, rising and falling in time with his breathing.

I stare out of my window and dream of angels.

PRAYING TO THE DEAD MICHAEL JACKSON

Heather Freckleton

When you're out for a long time doing things you don't like, I pray to Jesus and Santa but mostly to the dead Michael Jackson that Jed will come back. I imagine him striding up the road, his hair diving off in all directions like the brambles at the end of our back garden. Jed lived with us for three years and you said that though he wasn't my real dad, he was just like one. But that's not true as my dad's not real because he doesn't even have a name and Jed does. Jed is solid and tall and has green eyes with cinder-toffee flecks in them. He says I am probably an angel in disguise but the disguise is exceptional as my angel qualities don't always show. The best day ever was on the beach last summer when you and Jed covered yourselves in seaweed pretending to be a sea monster and chased me with the sand dragging at my feet and the sea rolling over like piles of blown leaves. Then I was between the two of you pulling at my arms and swinging me up again and again; the sun slanting into my face, hands being crushed and me screaming in excitement and pain. Later Jed carried me, my head on his shoulder and I ran one finger through the tiny curls that make his sideburns. He leaned over me to kiss you but I put my hand over your mouth and you blew a horrible wet sound on it and we laughed and I saw the black and red stripes of summer sky when I closed my eyes.

You said the only bad thing about Jed was that he'd given you the habit which was good at first because it stopped you worrying about everything. Things seemed thin, small and distant. You and Jed would share the smack in your bedroom and I never knew about it. But soon the smack stopped doing that and now you need more and more just to feel normal and to stop the big pains from taking over. Jed isn't here anymore and you have to get smack where you can and by doing things you don't like. You say that Jed will be away for up to a year but I don't think he'll leave us on our own for that long especially now that Michael Jackson is dead. Jed knows you love Michael Jackson and has seen you dancing to "Thriller" with your head thrown back and your arms like windmills. You once said Michael Jackson was like a god and so that's why I'm praying to him now for Jed to come back and for you to be happy.

You promised me spaghetti hoops tonight after school and that we'd snuggle up close on our shiny settee and watch *The Secret Garden*. But you got up this morning and your stomach cramps were like an octopus gone mad. Your eyes were dull and you forgot it was a school day and that I was still in my nightie with the crust of sleep on my face. I didn't think I could remind you that I'd been looking forward to our special tea and to cuddling up close, smelling your comforting smell and holding your hand. You had to go out. If you didn't score you might die. You always say this and though it hasn't happened yet, I could see myself, an eight year old stick of a girl, alone at your graveside wearing my new plastic sandals that might never tread a beach again.

Now I watch for you from the window. I hope you're not gone for ages like you were one day last week.

"Don't move," you'd said, "don't mess with anything and don't answer the door." My elbows were stuck to the table when you came back four hours later. I was so cold I couldn't smile at you. When you cooked up the smack, you made me a cup of tea and put three sugars in but forgot to make my dinner. You said the same thing again today and I know it's only because you want me to be safe and not get into any trouble. I hope you won't notice that I've put my school cardigan on over my nightie because I did have to go to my bedroom to get it. I went on tip-toe and didn't bang any doors so I'm sure no-one will know I'm in here while you're out. You're always telling me this is really, really important. Now my arms won't stick to the table while I'm waiting. It is quite boring so I'm imagining myself in the secret garden creeping through brambles that grab at my nightie and whip into my face. Then, just as it's getting dark and I'm feeling terrified and all alone, Jed jumps out and calls me a true angel for breaking the spell that has kept him there hidden from us all this time.

I can see Lee Shepherd now, coming up the street with his gran. She's shaped like the last pickled onion in a jar; sort of mottled and bloated looking as if a layer of skin is about to come off. You say it's because she's a secret drinker and that white cider makes her look pickled and is slowly dissolving her insides. I can see her food falling through all the empty spaces and right down into her legs. I'm not sure it's true about the drinking and you might have been trying to get your own back after she called you a smackhead and a bad mom. I thought it was a silly thing to say as it should be smackarm because that's where you inject it. You asked me whether I thought you were a bad mom and I felt so much love for you it was almost like a pain. Lee doesn't go to school much either. Nobody likes him, not even the teachers because he swears and fights and he can turn a funny colour. I think people are frightened of him, even his own mom and that's why his gran looks after him. I can see Lee's pale face looking this way but he doesn't wave.

The hours pass and I'm watching for you with nothing much in my mind except worry which makes me feel as if all the hairs on my head are made of electricity. But now I see you hurrying up the road, your head down hiding the painful, screaming need on your face. I'm so glad you're back and tap the window and wave but you don't look up. You come crashing into the house, keys skid and clatter across the table as you tear off your coat. You cook up the smack but don't make tea and I know the mad octopus will have nails on its feet by now. You sit on our shiny settee digging down the sides for the belt you tie round your arm. You treat your arm roughly as if you hate it; pulling the belt tighter and tighter. You flick your vein a few times so that it stands, purple and blue, a little round delicate hill on your arm. You whisper gently to the syringe as you put it in your vein and draw up blood to mix with the smack. And after making that little fountain out of the end of the needle you stick it carefully, so carefully back into your vein. I wonder why something that sounds so cruel can make you feel so much better. I know the real name for smack is heroin and I imagine a woman with long flowing hair rushing into the house to save you from pain. But it never happens and I know that this is the really cruel thing about it; pretending to be something it isn't.

Your head goes back and you say you must sleep. I watch you as you dream good dreams and a tiny dribble of spit slides slowly from one corner of your mouth. I sit next to you and hold your hand and send my thoughts out to you. Tonight we can have spaghetti hoops and after we've watched *The Secret Garden* we can watch the DVD of "Thriller" which will make you really happy. I look at the blank TV screen and see us reflected there. I pull my nightie down over my knees.

A LETTER TO MARTIN

Gillian Higgs

Larch Cottage
Little Weston
26 June

Dear Mr Amis,

On a visit to my local library a few weeks ago I counted five novels by Jeffrey Archer on the shelves and none by you. I can only surmise that this is because you have not obtained the "celebrity" status of one who has been publicly disgraced. As the librarian stamped my books, *Historic Gardens* and *Advanced Propagation,* I pointed out this literary omission.

"Well, Miss Wilson, you could order some Martin Amis should you so wish."

"I haven't got time to read novels," I told him, "far too much to do in the garden."

I was musing on the cult of regarding the infamous as famous as I drove home. Since retiring from teaching, a reluctant pensioner, I find myself increasingly puzzled by the ways of the world. Turning into my drive my attention was riveted by a tendril of *Convolvulus Arvensis* winding itself around the *Dicentra* Adrian Bloom. I suffered a momentary lapse of concentration and drove straight over the neighbour's cat, which habitually took dust baths on my flagstones.

I got out of the car to see if anything could be done for the creature. There were some bits of ginger fur welded on to my offside front tyre and I managed to peel a portion of his green plastic collar off the tread. Using a spade I scraped what little remained of the cat into a supermarket carrier bag. I quickly put the car away and popped the carrier bag into the Aga. My priority was to deal with the convolvulus before supper.

I was busy painting the leaves of this noxious weed with herbicide when my next-door neighbour Emma leaned over the fence, untidy blonde hair framing her flustered red face. She called out to me.

"Excuse me, Miss Wilson, but have you seen my cat Fluffy? He is ginger and is wearing a green collar."

This was very awkward. The last time we had spoken was in the late summer. I had been rather sharp to her on account of the *Chamerion Angustifolium* which she had allowed to invade her garden borders. It had flowered and the seeds were blowing into my rockery.

"Oh," she had said, "I thought it was a garden plant, the flowers were so pretty!"

I could not credit that anyone would think Rosebay Willowherb was anything but a weed and I had said as much to her at the time.

"Well," she had said, "I always say that life is too short to worry about the garden."

I had replied that that was obvious from the state of her borders. Mr Potter had kept that garden immaculate for forty years and it had taken just two years for this young couple to let it run to seed. Since then we had exchanged "good mornings" but that was all. On the spur of the moment I decided to conceal my part in the animal's demise. I offered sympathy and said I would keep a look out for him.

"Let me know if he turns up," I said.

At intervals during the evening I could hear her calling for her cat. I slept badly that night.

A week later Emma appeared in my garden while I was planting out some *Persicaria Vacciniifolium* on the edge of the rockery. The bright pink flowers give a splash of much needed colour in the autumn and early winter.

"I suppose you haven't seen anything of Fluffy? We miss him dreadfully and ..."

I watched, appalled, as she began to weep. I really had no idea how to cope with that sort of thing so I decided to distract her by offering a cup of tea. She sat at the kitchen table sipping her tea. She dried her eyes with the tissue I handed her, apologising for her breakdown.

"Pets become such a big part of your life; maybe it's hard to understand when you haven't got one."

"Oh I do know how you must feel. I would have loved to have a little pussy but at my age it wouldn't be fair, you know, if anything happened to me ..."

I don't know why I felt I had to lie to her. It seemed that once I had started I couldn't stop. I had always disliked cats, particularly Fluffy, after I saw him digging in the border I had just planted with Viola Clear Crystals. They were Mother's favourite pansy.

"I think it may be time to find another cat. It looks as if he is not coming home," said Emma. "It is hard not knowing what has happened to him, though."

"That's an excellent idea," I said briskly, "another cat will take your mind off him."

When Emma left she did something I wasn't expecting. She gave me a hug and said, "Thanks for being so kind Miss Wilson. Talking to you has made me feel a bit better."

I don't know why being hugged brought a lump to my throat.

One evening, about a week later, when I was getting out a packet of *Digitalis Purpurea* "Alba" to sow the next day, there was a knock on my door. Emma marched in, unhooked a small fawn-coloured kitten from her jumper and plonked it on the table. On the table! I would have to disinfect it later.

"This is yours," she said.

"Mine?" I repeated faintly.

"Yes, you could call her Minty after that plant on your front drive that Fluffy liked so much. Catmint, isn't it? Although I expect you call it by its botanical name."

"*Nepeta x Faassenii,*" I said.

"Oh, maybe not. Anyway, you have no need to worry about what will become of her in the unlikely event of anything happening to you because I would take care of it. I've got her brother. They are pedigree Singapuras. Aren't we lucky!"

She did a dance around the kitchen, too excited to notice my horror at this turn of events. She explained that I would have to put a litter tray down and gave me some kitten food and a catnip mouse.

"Must get back to my kitten, you can pay me in the morning."

In a daze I prepared a litter tray with a seed box and some peat and put food and water into two old saucers. How much did a pedigree cat cost I wondered? Fifty pounds? A thousand pounds? Anyway it was irrelevant because I would take it back in the morning, claiming that it made me sneeze.

The kitten watched me with interest. She had huge flat eyes and ears that looked too big for her head.

I sat down to read *Historic Gardens* but I found it hard to keep my eyes off the little creature. She remained on the table for a while, wetting her front legs with her little pink tongue and wiping her face with them! Then she jumped down and used the litter tray, continuing to dig until majority of the peat on was on the floor. Climbing the curtains occupied her for over an hour and I stood by, ready to catch her, terrified she would fall and hurt herself. Eventually she was worn out and she settled onto my lap and went to sleep, her thin little tail with its black tip curled around her body. I was afraid to disturb her so I sat there, finding it surprisingly pleasant to stroke her soft fur gently, until midnight, when she finally stirred.

I went to bed but did not sleep well. Muffled thuds, rustling and then a crash came from the hall downstairs. At 2am the kitten came into my room carrying the catnip mouse in her mouth. She jumped onto the bed and deposited it on my head before heading off into the bathroom for a fight with the toilet tissue. Then at 4am she climbed onto my bed again and snuggled into the nape of my neck, kneading me with her paws before falling asleep. I slept fitfully, afraid I might turn over and squash her.

She was still drowsy when I got up in the morning. She lay on her back, exposing soft, light-coloured fur on her little pink belly. I left her under the duvet and went to survey the damage. She had knocked a dried flower arrangement from the hall table and spread it around the house. Ears of wheat littered the kitchen floor. The little tinker!

The foxglove seeds were still on the table. I opened the dresser drawer, put them in and took out my cheque book. If I hurried I could get back from Emma's before my lovely Minty woke up for her breakfast.

Just a thought, Mr Amis, but if you are finding writing novels that no one reads an unrewarding occupation it may be that you, too, are ready for a complete change!

Sincerely yours,

Josephine Wilson.

THE BONESETTER'S NEPHEW

Alison Leonard

Cure. That's what they talked about when the bonesetter woman came near to the village with her pock-scarred nephew trailing behind her like a shadow. Might she cure the blacksmith's son's twisted leg? Yon growth on the cooper's neck, could she vanish it away? The stout stableman's wife as couldn't conceive – if she rubbed herbs together at midnight beside the holy well, like the bonesetter told her to, a littl'un would surely kick in her belly before the year was out.

But what could be the cure for nursing a baby not your own?

Lisette sat under the rustling poplars by the river, with the baby sleeping quietly in the crook of her arm, and wondered.

She'd been sucked into the life of this chateau and its village and estate last year, when Madame's final, least-wanted, baby arrived bawling on the scene. She soon learned that she had one job and one job only – to stop Madame's baby bawling.

Beside the broad river, watching the great barge float by carrying cognac down to the port, with its wash rippling behind it in a widening V, she was aware of the bonesetter's nephew walking towards her from the direction of the chateau. Afterwards, Lisette held in her heart the image of that brown rippling V. It was the image of her last moment of hope.

Mid-morning, and the sun not yet high in the sky, the shadow of the bonesetter's nephew met Lisette and the baby before the boy himself did. Everyone knew about the bonesetter's magic. But no-one except Lisette suspected that her shadowy nephew could make a different sort of magic. He followed the old crone around like a familiar: to the square where the maimed and the consumptive and the bilious formed an irritable queue for her services, to the gaps between fields where the old woman made fires to stir her potions, up into the forested hills where she'd disappear for the night. Lisette, who, like this disfigured silent boy, wandered the gardens and lanes in the course of her daily work, would find him collecting plants or muttering spells. He never smiled but gazed directly at her, his eyes like two clear marbles against the rocky surface of his scarred face. Each time she managed to meet his eyes, she felt calmer and her milk flowed more easily. Yet she'd never got to know his name or heard him speak a word.

His job was to hold the old crone's instruments and hand her the right one at the right time. Or, if she needed not something special in her hand but the right thoughts in her mind, she'd get him to sit by her in the dust at the roadside, where he'd go all dreamy while she was working her magic. Everyone thought the boy was simple. They'd mutter about the syphilis he must have caught from his dead mother, or call out, "Yer face got shot at by Mr Bismarck, then?"

They'd also murmur that if you dared to touch his scarred and pitted face, he'd heal you as well as the bonesetter would. But his skin was so grotesque, no-one could imagine laying a finger on it.

Yesterday, on the bonesetter's first visit for more than a year, she'd slipped the knife-grinder's arm-bone back into his shoulder before he could let the scream out of his wide-open mouth. Then she'd fetched two men from hay-making to hold down one of their sisters while she massaged the infant in the womb into the best position for birthing. Lisette had glanced at the nephew while the work was being done. He'd imitated the knife-grinder's readiness to scream, and then massaged his own belly while his aunt pressed and pummelled the unborn child into place. Each time, she'd seen him hold his breath during the process of the cure, then release it slowly as bonesetter and patient together came out of their trance.

The boy's shadow moved over Lisette and fell across the baby's face. The baby woke, and Lisette tightened her arm protectively under her chemise and urged the baby to the breast. But she couldn't resist looking sideways at the boy. All she could see was a dark silhouette, lit from behind by the blinding sun.

Blinking, she turned back to the baby, and as she turned, she heard a word come out of the bonesetter's nephew's mouth.

"Babby," he said.

Or did he? Had she imagined it? Was that sound actually a fish, risen from the river, plopping back in?

Whether he'd said it or no, she knew which baby he meant. He didn't mean this baby, the one she was feeding, Madame from the chateau's baby, Madame who paid Lisette's keep and a bit of small change over and above. He meant her own baby, the one she'd left at the farm cottage nine villages away, with the wet-nurse who'd four other babies to feed, half a dozen pigs clattering in and out through the squalid doorway, and filthy spitting pans dangling from thin hooks above the roaring fire.

She looked up again to where the boy had been standing. He wasn't there.

She stared all round her, as if he'd been a vision of angels.

But he hadn't vanished. He was standing in a little sandy break to her left, where the turf bank parted in a curve. He must have walked past her while the picture of her baby in the filthy farm cottage had been filling up her eyes.

He wasn't looking at her now. He was gazing at the flow of the river as it moved, strongly, glinting, towards the sun. She couldn't see his feet. Did he still have his boots on, the heavy boots he wore to walk the dusty lanes?

The baby had latched on and was guzzling fiercely. If only this was her baby, her own baby. If she'd been allowed, she'd have loved him as he needed loving. She shouldn't have left him with that woman. The baby's father had pushed her there.

"I'm a responsible man," he'd said. "I'll pay the midwife, and find you a position afterwards. I'll make sure you don't starve."

"But," she'd asked him, "what about our child?"

He'd scribbled the name of some agency, and when she told him the address they'd given her, instructed her which post-chaise to take. His goodbye, then, was final. Not even a kiss.

She didn't see the boy's plunge into the water. All she saw were glittering splashes, rising as high in the air as fireworks at the festival of Saint-Jean. Then the ripples, the circles, surging and stretching out to the bank, not only on her side, but to the other, the far side, too.

She watched, but the boy didn't emerge from the river. He'd vanished again while her eyes were clouded by visions of her own neglected child.

Lisette's breath stopped, and the baby stopped feeding and stared up at her, wide-eyed, as if as alarmed as she was.

She blinked, and suddenly he was standing before her, in water up to his waist, dripping. The skin of his face was not scarred and grotesque. It was clear as the skin of the baby in her arms.

"Dead."

The second word he spoke to her came together with the first, *babby*, and the two rang like bells in the cavern of her mind.

Babby dead. Dead babby.

Her own baby, among the other hungry babies, and the pigs, and the boiling spitting pans, was dead.

As Madame's baby latched onto the breast again, she knew that she'd sent her baby to his death in that farm cottage as surely as if she'd left him in the Paris street outside the House of Desire to be trodden into the cobbles by a horse.

In the split second that she stared into the face of the beautiful boy dripping with the brown water of the river, she knew it. His clear shining face gazed at her, and then slipped back down again under the ripples.

She was still. Even the baby in her arms lay still against her.

She looked at the circles in the river where the boy had sunk. He'd got his heavy boots on. He would sink forever. He had become beautiful just before her baby's death, and his own.

There was the low sound of mild splashing along to her left. It was the boy. He was clutching the turf of the bank, and, heavy with water through his clothes and in his boots, was hauling himself upright.

He stared at her, his face in full sun. It was pock-scarred, grotesque as before. Lisette laid the baby on the grass, buttoned up her chemise, and walked over to him to give him one brief kiss.

THE PERSISTENCE OF MEMORY, MR DALI

Helen Dalton

Every morning, the old man Oskar Drake would stroll down to the river to contemplate his existence. Every afternoon, he came to the conclusion that the task was impossible. By evening, he had already forgotten everything and by the next morning, the water would once again be his witness.

As the sun rose higher than ever before, seemingly in competition with herself, Oskar closed the back-door of his terraced house and pursued the path which chased gravestones through the churchyard to race's end; the river. The customary oaks, reddened through autumn's caress, greeted him with a flutter of their boughs. He saluted back with a military vigour. Directly ahead, the land sloped away towards the jetty where Oskar was accustomed to cogitate. Here he felt his memory crumple faster than the dying leaves cast off from the trees like rogue young.

Today felt different but Oskar could not fathom why. The river's waters, usually so impassively suited to his musings, seemed rather stagnant and sluggish. Squirrels, tawny red, flitted about not charmingly but irksomely. The air seemed to breathe reluctance, not introspective solitude. Whether his mood was replicating the atmosphere or vice versa was a moot point in Oskar's mind. He gently eased his groaning body down onto the edge of the landing stage and allowed his feet to whisper with the water. He forced his mind into the habitual trance but it would not come.

He started and looked behind himself as if startled by a sudden motion. The old man's mind was playing tricks on him again. He had shaken off the sharpness of youth many years ago. These days it took him long enough to remember what he had once done let alone the minutiae of the chronicles of German history which he used to teach and tend so well. Now even the slightest of noises had the ability to confound him and while he constantly lamented the banality of his existence, he knew subconsciously that it was safer.

In the distance a grey heron swooped down to the water and immediately soared to safety clutching its fishy prize in its yellow bill. Such dexterity and pace amazed the old man for whom the occupations of a day, from the mundane to the complex, had all become so much more wearisome. Now brushing one's teeth was as trying a riddle as deciphering nine down of the cryptic crossword. It was not that he felt dimmer, as if he had somehow unplugged a drain in his brain letting a horde of cells rush out, rather, the knowledge remained but one was compelled to grope about for it as if searching out a light switch in the dark until one's fingers clumsily grasped it and, bingo, illumination.

He sighed and heaved himself up. Today was not lending itself to circumspection. There was nothing for it but to retrace his steps back home and perhaps catch a programme on the radio. This he did like an automaton, approaching his dilapidated front door just as the bell tower of St. Oswald's next door struck twelve. Lunch time. At least it used to be, before his appetite had disappeared. Still, he might as well make a nominal gesture. He slotted his key inside the lock and gave the door a push. The wind blew him onto the leaf-strewn carpet of the hallway. A mammoth pile of prehistoric correspondence tottered on a low table. The faint stench of urine attested to the presence of a dog whose wet nose soon appeared around the corner of the entrance to the sitting room, swiftly succeeded by a slobbering tongue.

Oskar patted him on the head and continued on into the kitchen. The vast gallery window should have emitted a cascade of light but years of encrusted grime let through a mere trickle. Leaning towers of crockery were the monumental attractions of the region. The dining-room table at the centre of the room was strewn with the archaic remnants of long-forgotten newspapers whose stories were made history by the passage of time. A radio sat in the midst of the rubble, emitting the muffled murmurings of a Home Counties accent. There was a single chair at the head of the table facing the door where Oskar liked to sit and refuse the frazzled wiring of his brain in an attempt to rekindle the many memories borne there. Every inch of the floorboards, the brickwork, the furniture, was infused with a tantalisingly intangible sense of times past that receded each time Oskar reached out in earnest to grab them.

Thud. Bang. Thud.

The interruption shattered the deadened quiet of an old man steeped in solitude.

Bang. Bang.

His first thought was that the house was collapsing. It had been so long since he had had a visitor that he had forgotten the sound of a curious fist knocking at the door. He shuffled down the hallway, his dog leaping excitedly against the front door and exuding the energetic vim for life that Oskar no longer could.

"Get down, dog," he snapped. The name of the thing eluded him. He felt sure it was something witty but then he had always been a bit too esoteric for his own good.

Bang. Bang.

"Coming, coming," he shouted. Why were visitors always so damned impatient? It was as if the more quickly they arrived, the more quickly they could leave.

His trembling fingers gripped the door-handle and as the door swung open he stared blankly at the face of a young woman whose features seemed troublingly familiar.

"Hi Dad," she uttered with enthusiasm.

Oskar felt frightened. There were no children. His late wife, whose name temporarily eluded him, had not wanted to disturb the harmonious concord of their marriage with the wild roars of feral offspring.

"Why don't I come inside, Dad?" she suggested with forcefulness, easing past him into the corridor. "I wish you'd let me clean up in here."

Oskar turned slowly.

"No cleaning," he managed to croak. "I want everything to be as it was, so that I can remember it."

He entered the kitchen to find the young woman boiling the kettle and arranging tea-bags in twin mugs. The dog was sniffing her shoes and wagging his tail as if in recognition.

"I don't mean to be rude," he eventually ventured, "but who are you?"

As the girl turned around he saw only a quiet agony in her azure eyes.

"It's me, Dad, Georgie. Remember? I was here yesterday. In fact, I come to see you every day. We have arguments because you won't let me clean up."

Oskar was still puzzled.

"But I've never seen you before," he whimpered.

"It's okay, Dad, I'll help you to remember me. I'm Clara and Hugo's sister, Georgie. We all lived with you and Mum at Bank Cottage. We spent more time on the river at the bottom of the garden than we did in the house."

"Bank ... Cottage." Oskar tried out the words like an infant grasping for synonyms.

"My mother was Irene. You and she met in Germany after the war."

Oskar felt tears spring to his eyes and begin their treacherous descent across the tsunami of wrinkles that lined his face.

"My Irene, my beautiful Irene. We married last spring. She smiled at me in a dance hall in Berlin."

The young woman had moved forwards as the kettle screamed in a ghoulish frenzy behind her. She encouraged Oskar to take a seat at the table.

"Dad," she whispered, "Irene's gone. You were married thirty years and then you lost her. She passed away. I'm sorry Dad."

Oskar permitted the tears to wet his cheeks, and looked at the sympathetic woman.

"I know you," he said, caressing the contours of her face, "you're my naughtiest daughter, Georgie. You used to follow the milkman's cart in the mornings stealing bottles, until he convinced himself that he was losing his mind!"

Georgie smiled.

"I'm sorry. Sometimes I just … can't remember, that's all."

She squeezed her father's shoulder with affection.

"Now why don't you tell me all about how naughty I was while I make us both a cup of tea."

As Oskar began to talk of her childhood and she poured the hot water into the mugs, she allowed her tears to mingle with the tea.

THE CASE OF THE SIX SEEDS

Oliver Briscoe

Translator's note: I found this original Latin manuscript in a private Chester archive. I believe my translation to be generally accurate.

***

Dames are nothing but a truckload of headache when you're in my line of work. I'd hung up my hat and sandals, put the closed sign up and poured myself a glass of the good stuff from the bottom drawer.

This dame just came straight in and started talking at me. I held my hand up to stop her as I drained the glass, but she didn't take no notice of me. Dames never do.

She was a good looking broad. One of the best I've had in my office. Now I'd never be so stupid to say she was better than Juno, but this one was a real looker, for an older dame. Tall, black hair, green eyes that matched her gown. Looking tired and lost - anyone who comes to me usually looks like that.

I'd seen her around before, but I couldn't place her face until she was into her story. She wanted me to look for her daughter. She was babbling about fountains and messages and it hit me. She was Ceres and she wanted me to look for Proserpina.

I realised if I found the girl then I could get some kudos from the big guys on the mountain so I put down the drink and listened to Ceres. Apparently the dame had spent months searching high and low for her daughter.

Now this bit I already knew. All of us here on Olympus have our jobs to do. Me, I'm a messenger and the dame in front of me is in charge of crops. It's her job to make sure everything grows when it should and there is enough to go round for all the folks. But in all the time she's been mooching round, looking for her girl, she hadn't been doing her job.

She was telling me that she'd been sitting listening to a fountain yesterday who told her that Pluto had taken Proserpina to the Underworld. She wanted me to go and ask for her girl back. I held up my hand to stop her and spoke.

"Pluto? Now listen here, little lady. It may say "Mercury, Messenger" on my door, but I don't take messages anywhere. And I ain't going to see him in the Underworld. You can't pay me enough, lady, to take a trip down there."

The dame turned on the waterworks and I ain't nothing but a sucker for a crying doll, so I promised her I'd go and see Pluto the next morning.

***

I hate the Underworld. It's just so grey and flat. And then there's old man Pluto himself. I guess he's my uncle, but this family ain't what you could call close. Some call him prickly and you have to make sure you don't annoy him when you're down there otherwise you won't be needing sunglasses for a few months, if you catch my drift.

Now if you've never met him, and I hope for all your sakes you haven't, I've got to tell you that Pluto really does live up to his image. He's a big lad. And he's got the blackest beard you ever saw. Black hair too, and thick black eyebrows. We can pick any shape and size we like - so I guess Pluto must like this one.

But there's one problem I have with the old man of the Underworld. The guy likes me. He calls me Merc, which I hate. Always wants to talk, to get the skinny on what's happening topside.

And it's always the grimy, seedy gossip he wants. Try and tell him about Jupiter's new plans and he cuts me off with a wave, but start telling him about what Juno said about Minerva to Diana and the guy's on the edge of his seat. And then there are the card tricks. Pluto sits down here all day practising card tricks. His hands are big and clumsy and he can't really do them. But what can you do? Unless you can tell him how amazing his tricks are then you'll find yourself rowing on the Styx for a month or two.

Normally when I've been down to see him he's been alone but this time there was a pale, thin girl next to him. Proserpina, I guessed. She wasn't smiling and didn't look like she had smiled for a while.

"Oh Mercury," she said. "Has mother sent you?"

Pluto cut her off with a wave. "Hush, child. I want a word with my old pal Merc. Then we'll find out what he's here for." He smiled at her and to my surprise she smiled back. Perhaps there's more to this than meets the eye.

The big man grasped my elbow and manoeuvred me to the corner of the room. I held my breath, waiting for the first terrible card trick. Pluto fixed me with those dark eyes of his and said, "Ceres has sent you, hasn't she? You've come down here to take my sunshine away, haven't you?"

"You don't know the trouble you've caused topside by taking her."

He looked surprised. "Trouble? What kind of trouble?"

"Man, it's bad up there. This girl and her mother are in charge of planting all the crops and making sure they grow. Well, nothing's been planted this year. Ceres has been searching for the girl because she needs her help and she's been too heartbroken to work. There's nothing to eat anywhere. The people are blaming Jupiter, and he's blaming Ceres and she's blaming you. Why did you do it, old friend?"

"Oh Merc, you don't know what it's like for me down here, do you? You can't. You're funny and witty and can travel anywhere and the girls fall over you. Me, I'm rough and gruff and stuck down here in the dark and the gloom. It gets so lonely down here, you know, Merc, so sometimes I go up to a place on the top and watch the girls bathing."

OK. So this is getting weird and creepy, even for Pluto.

"Look, I know it's wrong, but I can't help it. Anyway, one day I saw Proserpina there. She was the most beautiful thing I'd ever seen, and before I could change my mind I grabbed her and brought her down here."

I asked the question I needed to. "Have you … ?"

Pluto interrupted me. "No, not yet. I want it to be right."

That's one less thing the girl and I would have to explain to her mother.

Pluto carried on. "But Merc, she's won't eat anything down here. She's wasting away."

"Are you surprised, old friend? You know the rules. If she eats down here she stays."

"I know, Merc. I've tried tempting her with everything, you know. I even found a pomegranate, the only fruit down here, the other day and gave it to her. She just looks at it all day."

"So what's it to be? Keep her here and let her and everyone topside starve, or let me take her back to her mother and we'll all be happy. And you never know, old friend, she might want to come back of her own will one day."

Pluto sighed and looked at his big hands. Then he said "OK, then. Take her back. Just let me say goodbye."

We turned back to the girl by the throne. And I noticed Proserpina put down the pomegranate with a bite missing, then pretend she was clearing her throat to spit out a mouthful daintily. All class, these posh dames. But I thought I'd better keep quiet about what I'd seen.

Pluto went up to her and said something. I could have listened in. I have the sharpest ears in town. But I turned my head and left them to it. I heard Proserpina say "thank you" loud enough for me to hear too so I looked back to find her in a surprisingly tender embrace with the big man. I'll never understand dames, you know. He's kidnapped her, kept her in this gloom for six months, starved her and now she hugs him goodbye.

And then, as I was taking her back up top, I asked her about the pomegranate.

"Did you swallow any of it?" I said to the dame, looked at her straight.

"Only six seeds, I was so hungry."

I stopped and held her by the shoulders and made her look at me. "You silly girl. You'll have to spend six months of every year down here now, you realise."

She looked back at me and said, with great finality, "Oops. Silly little me! Oh well." And gave me a little grin.

Like I said, dames are a mystery to me.

DREAMTIME PROVIDENCE

Lynne Voyce

James's soft whispers and guttural moans evaporated into the vast outback like summer rain. We clung to each other in the emptiness. The sweating groundsheet under us; our campfire just a patch of ruby embers in the dirt; billycans stacked clean under the flysheet; flagon empty, ready to be refilled at the next bar.

It was 2am. We were camping about fifty miles from anywhere, sharing an army surplus tent, cooking on a Bleuet: couldn't afford a motel. After walking all day, hypnotized by the solitude, we'd stayed up late: played cards, drank beer, and ate steak and beans, laughed so hard I couldn't catch my breath.

After making love we went to our separate zed beds still connected, comfortably silent, pulling the pest nets over us.

But as I lay in my straitjacket sleeping bag, feet throbbing, head pounding, the pitch dark took on sharp edges. Every time James's raw snore filled the tent and subsided, the pain in my temples grew keener. I took some comfort that at least in the morning, when I unzipped the tent, I would be queen of all I surveyed; free to taste the wilderness in any way I pleased. I thought about the team back home: the girls tied to the alarm and the day-in-day-out of work; collecting bags of blood and wiping arses in the claustrophobia of the city; watching old women fade away.

I had to get outside where the sky stretched over the infinite scrub; feel the stillness. Too often I had bad dreams.

I slid off the bed, pulled down my sleeping bag, put on my jeans, wet with sweat from the day's hike and pushed my feet into unlaced boots. It was a cold night in the desert, the heat of the day having fled into the clear skies but I wanted the chill to embrace me; I wanted to feel part of my surroundings. Half naked, I fastened a tool belt around my waist and fetched the metal detector from the back of the Combi. I'd been a treasure hunter all my life; never found more than fake trinkets and tin cans though. Maybe this time I'd be lucky, dig up a relic, donate it to a museum; see my name on a plaque.

I started slowly, concentrating on the head of the detector gliding over the night-drenched sand. But after ten minutes I was moving fast, numbed by the ocean of emptiness, the mystic hum of the suddenly silent night. I circled the tent, casting out a hopeless thought with each revolution. Then, just as my mind reflected the emptiness around me, the piercing persistent bleep of the detector shot into the air, crying out for attention. I stopped, swept the detector back and forth - a soft, low sound building to a scream.

I punched the heel of my boot into the sand to make a mark, deadened the beep then drew the trowel that hung limp at my waist, as an ageing gunslinger would a revolver - expecting to lose. I knelt and dug, tossing the sand to either side. About half a metre down I heard the clang of metal. I flicked on the torch with my free hand, scooped sand off the surface of whatever I'd struck; then shone the beam into the hole to see the dull colour of gold at its depths. My breath caught and danced a steady path into my forehead making me giddy. At last I had found something, a gold nugget, maybe worth enough for James and I to stay in a motel next time, make love in a bed.

I reached down with one hand and tried to pull it out, expecting it to give like a ripe potato but it wouldn't budge. Maybe it was stuck to a submerged rock, just the tip of a worthless iceberg. I tried to dig around it but I couldn't. Then I dropped the torch, threw myself onto the ground, stomach against the still warm sand, reached down, easing my hands either side of the object, feeling the earth cold against my fingers, then a myriad of sharp edges. I braced and pulled.

It was heavy work, reminded me of my father delivering calves on the farm. I closed my eyes; saw him grinning with pride, pulled harder. At last it was out, born into that sultry night in the desert, shining in the beam from the discarded torch - a huge gold nugget, the size of a football, thirty-five, maybe forty pounds. Crystalline gold, the purest form of naturally-occurring gold in the world. I knew it. I was a prospector.

I lay there for a moment, comparing my discovery with the full moon, lying on the dark blue surface of the night, feeling what can only be described as a gold rush, a hundred years on from Klondike.

The faint possibilities rained down like thousands of fluttering dollars: James could leave the factory, start a furniture business; I could go back to college, maybe qualify as a real nurse. We could move to the suburbs, buy a new wagon, go to Europe. But these weren't dreams: they were hopes, already tempered by reality. What I needed was a brazen, dare-to-imagine, technicolour dream.

In the west, shimmering like the rock in my arms, was Venus, the brightest object in the sky, save for the moon.

"I will call you "The Evening Star"," I whispered to my prize, "because you came to me in the night." Then I stood and walked along the trail of light from the torch, back to the tent, the Evening Star against my naked chest, like a suckling child.

I ducked into the tent where James was still snoring. The noise filled the space but now it was the gentle sighs of my husband: reassuring, comfortable. I bent over, kissed his sweating forehead, still holding my find in both arms. I took a towel from the metal rack at his feet; wrapped up the gold, put it in the rucksack under my zed bed, then lay back to watch the shadows on the tent's apex and dream. What next?

But no answers came to me in the outback - no blinding dreamtime epiphany. I had expected solutions: the only things that came were questions. I had things to treasure: James, the girls on the ward, a kinship with every up-against-it skivvy in the city, but, with sudden wealth, would they all be lost to me? And as I was now richer than my wildest dreams - what were my wildest dreams? The only real dream I'd ever had had already been taken. Perhaps I didn't deserve another, having allowed myself to be worn into an empty, dreamless vessel.

And the buried memories surfaced so much easier than my prize had. Momentarily it was the child I had lost and still longed for. My child: that was taken before its first big-mouthed breath. He belonged to God now. But the Evening Star belonged to me. It was meant for me: a piece of fate directed by the pinprick stars above my head.

I got up early the following morning, woke James, packed the Combi; then we drove back to the city, singing songs. James knew nothing of the Evening Star, yet he still sang, still smiled, and still laughed at my silly jokes. He looked young and happy, the perpetual frown of city life having disappeared. Everything felt OK. And as I swung the Combi into the drive, "Freefallin'" on the radio, I realised what I had to do.

At 2am, when James was asleep and the city had slowed to near standstill, I went out to the back of our house; the nearly-new moon shone onto our unkempt urban garden, thirsty from neglect, overlooked by the neighbours' bedroom windows. I stole quietly to the shed, took a spade and went to the end where our land meets the railway embankment. A scrappy wire and wood fence marked the boundary. A freight train rattled past, its beams catching the slats of the fence. I ducked, held my breath, tried to sink into the night-time shadows cast by ever-present light pollution. But everyone was asleep and soon the reassuring stillness of night was once again uninterrupted.

I struck the black earth with the spade and dug. I'd wanted to do the same that night a year ago; put the little alien baby that I'd scooped from the bathroom floor in a shallow garden grave, marked with a lolly-stick cross. Like a pet. So no-one else need know. So I could be spared the pity and embarrassment. So I could talk to the dead bones any time I needed.

But James had called an ambulance before I'd broken trance. Before the blood and mess had been wiped off the tiles.

Once the hole was deep enough I placed the Evening Star, still wrapped in the towel from the Outback, back in the earth, covering it with soft dark dirt, murmuring the Lord's Prayer as I did. I would come back to it one day, when I could – when I'd found a new dream.

HIGH FLYER

Sophie Coulombeau

"How did he look?"

"He was a good-looking lad," said the maître d'. "One of those very good-looking Asian boys."

"But how did he look that day? Frightened? Determined?"

"Oh," said the maître d', and pressed his thumb into one closed eye and his index finger into the other, as if perhaps keeping his eyeballs in their sockets might keep his two small sleepy sons safe in their beds at home for all time, "he looked like a lad with the world at his feet."

The girl with the basket, hurrying through Sainsbury's, stopped. She turned, and walked back to the newspaper stand, and stared at the front page. For a few moments she stood slack-jawed, her basket hanging limply from one hand. Then she took out her phone and texted. HAVE U HEARD HAVE U HEARD. Too urgent for kisses.

"He bought a magnum of Cristal," said the girl at the bar with the black spiky eyes. The eyes were dry. She had seen worse things in Sarajevo. "But, you know, he always did." A pause. "I have never known such a big tipper," she added reverently. "Today, the same as ever."

"And how many glasses?"

She thought, tapped her tooth with a talon. "One. I thought that was weird."

"He was a real high flyer," said the ex-headmaster, who sat in his garden, pickled brown by retirement. "I don't know what else to say."

"Nice suit," said the bloke who had been in the lift. "I know a nice suit when I see one. Lovely cut." He sipped the coffee in the Styrofoam mug and stared at the table. "We didn't talk. I mean, you don't, in the lift."

"No comment," said the chief executive.

"Mr. Jopling, can you at least tell us -?"

"No comment," he said. As the elevator doors closed, sealing him in a cold cocoon of black marble, he sponged the sweat from his hairline with a hanky.

"I thought you said you didn't really know him," said her boyfriend, watching her from the kitchen doorway.

"I didn't, but it's still weird."

"Why? Happens to people every day."

She made a helpless, angry gesture with the clump of celery in her hand. "It's weird because I met him. Because I know people who know him. And because he was so – the golden boy."

"Right," he said, and his eyes were hard.

She slammed the fridge door.

"We wondered when this would happen," said the journalist. "You can only say 1929 so often before some poor bugger joins the dots."

He swallowed the last dribble of wine and his Adam's apple bobbed like a nodding dog. He slammed his glass on the table a little too hard. "Still," he said, to his own

collar more than anyone else, "never thought he'd be so young."
"It was a nice morning," said the waiter. "We're famous for the view. I didn't think anything of it."

"I'm not surprised," said the German guy who'd agreed to go off the record. "It's about time people realized what it's like. You're sitting at your desk, and someone around you picks up the phone, then they go upstairs, and ten minutes later they come back down with a box, and clear their stuff, and that is it. Two minutes ago you were talking about the football, and then that is it. It happens every day. Nobody knows who will be next."

"One for the ladies," said the maître d'. "Always here with a girl. But never the same girl twice." A stillborn chuckle bubbled in his throat as he remembered bare throats and puffed-up breasts, perfumes and ankles and hair bobbing, bouncing, swishing.

"That wasn't it," said the girlfriend. "That wasn't it at all."

"The reading," said the chaplain, "will be from Tennyson's *In Memoriam.*"

"TRAGIC WASTE" screeched the Evening Standard.

***

He stepped into the lift and smiled at the bloke in the corner, who didn't look up from his *London Lite*. The numbers blinked one to eighteen, and he stepped out at the restaurant floor. The maître d' wasn't there. He waited for a minute or two, and then walked through the crystal clinking and babble of the restaurant, straight to the bar. He asked for a magnum of Cristal and one glass, and the girl filled a bucket with ice, with a faint air of hangover. She picked a clump of mascara from her eyelashes as she swiped his card for the tab.

He walked out onto the terrace into the sun, the waiter following with his champagne bucket. It was still early, and a morning chill lingered in the air. The terrace was quiet. The waiter half-bowed and pocketed his fiver, and went back inside.

He had always liked the quiet at this height. The bleed of city noise - the blare of traffic, babble of voices, slapping symphony of footfalls, ringtones, rasping of dogs and joggers - all smoothed away to a muted hum. The stirring of the breeze, the caw of a bird, were the only real sounds.

He straightened his tie, and loosened his collar, still stiff from the press this morning. He touched each cufflink once, like a charm.

He took the neck of the bottle, glittering with icy droplets, in one hand, and lifted it free of the bucket. Then he tipped it to his mouth and took a long, deep gulp. The bubbles surged up his nose and he choked and sneezed at the same time. He wiped his mouth carefully with a tissue before continuing, and then folded the tissue and put it in his pocket.

He stood up on the wall. The railing pressed vainly at his knees.

The City lay spread beneath him, spires and domes and sheaths of glass windows packed like dominoes. A flock of pigeons wheeled about the great ribbed breast of St Paul's. Trails of people twitched on the street below, cars twinkled in the sun. The great flash of the river stained his eyes white, but he could just make out the distant high rises of the south, swaddled in films of blue.

From the feeling that it was the right thing to do, he spread his arms out wide. The bulbous bottle clutched in his right hand seemed, in his mind's eye, somehow fitting; a flashing growth on the tiny human star that could have been seen from the street below if anyone had looked up.

But nobody looked. The maître d', the girl at the bar, the bloke in the lift, the waiter, the anthill of London below, all pared their fingernails and looked at the floor at that precise moment. Across the world, those who knew him burped or put the phone down or finished their coffee.

Already, as he leaned forward into the vacant air, he thought of what they might say.

WELLY BOOTS

Jan Bengree

Yesterday a family legend bit the dust.

My late Aunt Sal always wore black wellies. And yesterday, while clearing her stuff, I chucked them out. But as I chucked them, something fell from them.

All through my childhood, Aunt Sal came for tea on Sundays. On arrival, she'd sit on our step, dragging those boots off so the rubber made sort of farting noises. Sometimes Sal put the boots on again because Aunt Flo demanded a repeat performance. Flo loved repeat performances. And that thought tickled them both, but that thought made Dad blanch.

The Aunts guffawed. They liked farting boots. They liked repeat performances. They became uncontrollable: both Aunts and the farting of boots.

Flo wasn't my real aunt. She was Sal's friend. Dad said they shared a love of farming. Mum said it was more basic than that. Flo wore Green Flash pumps splattered with chicken feed, flour and something brown like dead blood. She was pink faced, blue eyed and in certain lights, had the look of a cherub. But blonde Flo was A Dark Horse. Dad said.

They worked on a farm. Sometimes I'd help milk cows. They wore dungarees and lived in a barn like the chalet of Heidi's Grandfather. It had one bed containing two pairs of pyjamas. They were striped with cords round waists and baggy legs. The room reeked of tobacco. Flo reeked of pear drops. Sal had a moustache. Once I saw a shred of marmalade glittering in it. It stayed there all day.

***

The Family came each Sunday. They were Dad's Side. Mum was an orphan. She had just Dad and me. She liked that. She said we were a trio holding the world at bay. I didn't want to hold the world at bay. I wanted to leap into it, no holds barred.

So, every Sunday the Family clattered up our path. There was Sal, Flo, Nan, Gramps, Aunty Lou, Uncle Peter, their daughter Rose. Sal and Lou were Dad's sisters. Rose was my younger cousin who passed exams. This was mentioned constantly. She brought homework to tackle quietly in corners. Rose spoke quietly too; whispering words, like secrets into a wishing well. Everyone listened to Rose. I made a note to speak quietly myself. I saw it was a good ploy.

And there was also my elder cousin Gloria.

***

As they arrived, I flung coats on banisters. Nan's was fur. It smelled of scent, mothballs and face powder. Gramps had a donkey jacket, smeared with plaster and speckled with cat hairs. Once a picture of a naked woman fell from the pocket. It was ripped from a magazine. I left it by the banisters on purpose.

Nan shrieked. "I thought you'd got over that malarkey, Sidney!"

Nan's shriek was a playground whistle.

"What a beauty, Pops!" said Sal. "Fancy keeping HER in your pocket!"

"You next, Gloria!" said Flo, patting Gloria's behind with relish.

And I watched Sal turn as white as the icing on Mum's ginger cake.

So Dad shepherded everyone in and Mum dragged curlers from her hair, curved on lipstick.

"Rest your bones," she said, "I'll fiddle in here." And she hid in the scullery, putting doilies on plates, adding angelica to sherry trifle, while everyone's coats hung perilously on our banisters.

***

Later, Mum served ham salad, bread, butter, and well-brewed tea.

After pudding, Flo sang Negro songs. Flo said they "reached her" because she herself was someone on society's edge who knew injustice. Flo sang about Slaves and Masters. We weren't an emotional family (feelings rarely expressed) but as Flo sang, Nan did copious dabbing to her nose with Stratton powder puff and Mum did fussy things to a teapot. And Gramps stood whistling in the doorway, hands in pockets, trousers stretched out wide like jodhpurs.

Sometimes Flo wept. Her singing became more gasp than song. It seemed Flo's leanings had once been sidetracked into marriage, but Sal had straightened her out. And Flo's tears were often those of relief.

"They're besotted with each other," Gramps said.

"They're devoted to each other," Lou said.

"And they're together," Peter said.

"We must accept Flo," Nan said, "or we'll lose our Sal." And she clicked on with her knitting as they weighed up her words while our kettle boiled.

***

One Sunday there was An Atmosphere.

Mum chivvied Sal. "Settle yourself at table. And you, Flo."

But Flo gazed at Gloria, and it seemed she couldn't stop this gazing. And a preening Gloria glittered round, pouting her lips and fluttering her eyelashes, while misty-eyed Sal fiddled with the cruet, and salted intricate patterns onto Mum's white tablecloth.

Flo was truculent. She glared at the cats, glared at Dad. She stared harder and harder at Gloria. So Dad, speechless and hands fiercely clutching his braces, quivered with disapproval. And Mum hid in the scullery, in her fluffy violet slippers.

That particular Sunday was Gloria's seventeenth birthday. She glowed.

"Bit of alright," said Gramps.

"Coming up womanly," said Uncle Peter.

Aunt Flo's voice was husky. She savoured her trifle. She licked jelly off her spoon.

"Yes." Her voice slithered into cream on her trifle top, "wonderful bones, and sculpted calves. A Rodin dream! "

"Flo's ARTY!" Nan hissed. "She knows about calves, knows about Rodin."

Flo smirked, winked at Gloria. The room hushed.

"Hmm. I'll put the cats out," said Mum.

"I'll have a smoke," said Dad.

So, as Sal slumped further into her chair, we sat in silence because suddenly there seemed no choice.

And Mum (back with a tea tray and scowling at Flo) cooed. "They're teasing, Sal!" And trifle plopped off my spoon and jelly gurgled rudely in my dish.

Then Mum patted Sal's cheek in passing and Gloria sashayed away on stilettos and Flo's eyes shone as though lit by candles.

***

That night, Mum and Dad talked outside my room.

"Don't fret," whispered Mum, "Gloria's a honey pot. Boys love her. And Flo won't leave Sal."

Dad gruffly agreed, shuffled to the bathroom.

But Mum stayed alone on the landing. And she was weeping.

***

The next Sunday: "Where's Flo?" asked Mum.

"Fish to fry," said Sal. Her boots were fartless on our step.

"Where's Gloria?" asked Dad.

"Some lad," said Rose. Her voice was shrill on our step.

So Mum settled Sal with the *Express* and three cream cakes and smiled her anxious smile and showed the blueness of her eyes.

Then everyone's minds worked overtime.

"NOT our Gloria!" croaked Lou. She twisted a purple hankie between her fingers.

"NOT our Gloria!" bellowed Peter. He screeched off in his red Cortina.

And Sal lay prostrate on Mum's candlewick bedspread, while Dad and Gramps smoked Players by the hen hut.

"What a palaver!" said Gramps.

"A right to-do!" said Dad.

So Aunty Lou was tucked in my bed, compress on forehead, curtains drawn, daughter Rose beside her (cocking sly looks at a list of Irregular French verbs).

And Mum sighed. "It's a different world nowadays …"

And Dad, slurping his tea and forgetting he'd ever accepted Sal and Flo, yelled, "NOT under MY roof!"

Later, I found Mum in the garden: in pink dress, fluffy violet slippers. Mum, sitting quietly by her lilacs.

Of course Sal and Flo split eventually. But Gloria married, had sons, a string of rugby-playing lovers. Sal remained by herself.

And Flo met Eileen, who also sang folk-songs.

"Sal will always mourn Flo," said Dad.

So Sal stayed alone till she died.

***

Then yesterday, under Sal's bed, I found photographs of folk long gone. There were my parents and grandparents: Nan in fur, Gramps in donkey jacket. Mum, Dad, Lou, Peter. I stuffed some pictures in my bag. Dad cricketing, me swimming. And there was Flo before the split: holding kittens, sipping beer, dancing a Fling, and singing her songs of Injustice.

But I found far more photos of someone else.

I found them beneath Sal's sink, lurking in the farting wellies. And I remembered Sal on our step, remembered ancient Sundays. But the wellies had to go. I hurled them towards stuff assigned for binning. And something fell out: photos, tied in ribbon. And I couldn't believe what I saw.

There was Mum, in curlers, on a swing. There was Mum, flowers in hair, running by the sea, sitting in woods. There was Mum in those fluffy violet slippers. There were so many pictures of Mum I stopped counting. I found a close-up. And I saw Mum: serene, so beautiful. And I flipped it over; saw Mum's spidery writing: *To Darling Sal. Remembering Our Special Love. xxx*

So yesterday I learned something. And I was moved.

As one family legend bit the dust (Sal's exclusive love for Flo) I discovered a new one. But this one shall stay secret.

Aunt Sal would be glad. My Mum would be glad. Very.

AND SPEAKING OF SILENCE

Emily-Jo Hopson

My mayr grew round in the middle, and her feet swelled up so big she had to sit down all the time. And my father, he spoke to her belly in Russian, and my mayr talked to it as she walked to town, and as she did the dishes, and as she dusted the shelves, and as she tucked her baby girl into bed at night. Sometimes in Armenian, sometimes in English. Sometimes she was sure it spoke back, gurgling sentences in three different languages. Other times it just kicked. In the end her belly burst and out flooded water and more water and myself.

As a girl she inserted herself into visions of grey stone universities. She promised that she would never, not in a thousand years, spend a day as her mother did; sweating in kitchens of brown broth, burning her fingers on flat breads, crying over onions. But she came to America and married a Russian man, and decided to save her dreams for after her first child was born, and after she was raised; when the first child was six years old she decided to save her dreams for after her second child was born, and raised. So she spent her days, many of them in our kitchen, burning her fingers on flat breads, crying over onions. Mayr can name every country on the map, and she makes the best boeregs. She can quote from books I've never heard of, and she remembers birthdays.

I spent most of my fourteenth birthday kissing a girl with lips the colour of earthworms. Her name I've forgotten, but her lips I remember, being the first lips I ever kissed that way. She wished me happy birthday with those lips and then she kissed me, in my parents' bathroom, in my parents' house. I grinned so much my teeth got in the way.

I gripped her elbows until she stopped kissing me and wiped her mouth.

"You'll get better with practice," she said, and left.

The next girl made my eyes burn and my ears throb at the same time. She left red hairs on my shirt every time we hugged, and on my pillow when she lay on my bed and talked and talked and talked until I couldn't remember where she started or how she got to where she was. She taught me how to tell stories without minding whether anybody wanted to hear them. She talked and talked to my mayr, my father, my sister, my cat. On and on she talked, and it rushed out all at once like beads on thread. When she wasn't storytelling, she was eating or kissing. I listened and ate and kissed with her until she married. I went to the wedding - the place behind my eyes burned, my ears throbbed. Do you know, when she wasn't there, I felt the silence like lead boots? I wore it like a helmet; I pushed my hands into it like gloves.

And speaking of silence, on snow days my father wrapped himself and me and my sister up in the warmest clothes we had and laid bright orange flowers grown in greenhouses on his father's grave. It was so cold they seemed to glow, orange on white on brown on blue. He said they would keep the old man warm. To my sister he gave bouquets of small flowers from the house to make necklaces and bangles for the marble angels; to me he gave water and rags to fill the vase and clean the stone. When I was five I got lost there. It was spring, the stones looked the same. I walked the wrong way, my father was north and I went south, I thought I saw him. I stood at the grave of a stranger and cried and cried until my mayr found me. I laugh now; I think I thought I was lost for good. And every time we came home from warming the grave, my grandmother gripped my father's hands and spoke Russian to him.

Her funeral was in September. I watched my sister flush red as she cried in public and my mayr gripped my father's shoulder. I watched the grave fill up bit by bit. They found her in the chair in the corner of the kitchen; her skin was still warm, in her lap a bowl of potatoes for peeling. I watched them watch the body for hours when she went. My dad was silent, my mayr was crying, my sister was listening to the radio upstairs. After the funeral, Father excused himself and went for a walk. I followed him. He walked until nobody but me could see where he was. Nowadays I forget my father's face from time to time, but never the man he met with. I was ten, he was young, he held my father's wrists the way my mayr held his hands, he hugged him the way my mayr hugged him, there was no mistake, they kissed. What did I think? I hid behind a tree. A bird was singing. I picked up a stone. My father turned around - I didn't wait to see if it was dead, I ran back to my mayr. I never told her. I began to notice the man in other places. He walked past our house, he waited outside my father's place of work, and he paid his respects to a dead man two graves over as we buried him.

I woke up with a feeling in my chest, the day my father died. I looked down. The sheets fluttered; my ribs pushed up under them in beats of three. Pushpushpush. I turned over toward the nightstand. I didn't know yet that he was dead. Each capillary trembled in my hands. I pushed my fingers into the silence; I slid my heavy feet toward the foot of the mattress. Pushpushpush. The front of the house rocked. I'd never noticed before that wind moves like water, one wave came in the wake of another. Did our cat tie herself around my feet? Pushpushpush. I've never felt anything like it since, if I felt it then; the air fell out of me like a door was opened, I felt like my lungs would turn inside out. My hair stuck to my throat, I think I thought about my mayr running a brush through hers, her mayr scrubbing her shoulders - the clock in the kitchen behind my grandmother's body ticking, marking the seconds she'd been dead, the shadows that lengthened in the hours after her husband died.

Did I think about my father's lover in the background of our photographs? (One Father wanted me to take, '53: he stood outside a café; the Lover sat in the window. They are secretly side by side. I have it with me, here. Look. Others he appeared in without my knowledge, others before I knew he existed.) I thought about changing the weather when I was a child, I tried to stop the wind; I thought about the talking girl, I concentrated until my lips were numb, but one wave came in the wake of the wake of the wake of another. Pushpushpush. I lay awake in bed and didn't know my father was dead, as he had lain awake and not known his father was dead, as his father had lain awake the same, with our dead parents' blood in our veins. Downstairs my mayr slept beside her dead husband. A clock on the dressing table marked the seconds.

PENGUINNAPPED!

David Diggory

We were sitting in the classroom at the Bluecoat School, Yolanda and I. The sun was still streaming in, though it was late on this hot August afternoon. Beside us was a penguin.

"Yolanda," I began, "how could you do this?"

We'd been to Chester Zoo for the afternoon. The students in my charge had enjoyed clicking their digital cameras. They'd wandered among the animals, gazing at the orang-utans, gawping at the jaguars, gasping at the spectacled bears.

I'd told them about the spectacled bears in my preparatory lesson.

"The spectacled bear," I'd advised, "lives in Venezuela. It is hunted, for the farmers believe it kills their stock. In fact, it is a scavenger, like a vulture."

One had to be careful, using technical words like "scavenger," for these were Spanish language students - 14 to 17 year-olds - here to attend a summer school, and learn a bit of English.

I'd also told them about the penguins. The Humboldt. The kind they kept at Chester Zoo. The very kind that was now sitting on my desk.

"Well, the feeder -" began Yolanda.

"The "keeper"," I corrected her.

"The keeper was feeding the birds."

"Excellent use of the past continuous, Yolanda. Do go on."

"The keeper was feeding the birds, and I stepped in to help."

Feeding time at the penguin enclosure could be a raucous affair. It was easy to imagine Yolanda slipping into the enclosure, during the confusion.

"She invited me," added Yolanda, correcting my surmise.

" "Invited," Yolanda?" Her tenses were impeccable, but one had to be careful with definitions.

"Yes."

"And then what?"

"When it was all over, I took the penguin."

The casualness of her explanation was beginning to grate.

"But, why?"

Here was the crux. My lesson that morning had suggested, if anything, that a penguin is far safer in its enclosure than it is in the outside world. Humboldts are under threat: from the weather, and from Man. El Niño causes upwelling currents in the Pacific to cease; those currents carry nutrients on which fish - and *ergo* Humboldts - depend. Absence of current means absence of fish. Furthermore, overfishing of anchovies off the Chilean coast can leave Humboldts starving.

And if those factors don't constitute enough threat, there is the issue of the guano …

The kids had really got into the guano.

I'd presented my celebrated imitation of a Humboldt, settling to squat.

"Now, what do all houses possess?" I'd asked.

"Swimming pools." That had been Laura's suggestion.

"Maybe in some parts of Spain," I'd replied, patiently. "Not here in England. Not everywhere."

"Air conditioning?"Now it was Pedro, piping up.

Same answer.

Eventually, after further gyrations to demonstrate the Humboldts' evacuation method, my students had cottoned on.

"Toilets!"

"And what if there aren't any toilets, anywhere? What is the consequence, through thousands upon thousands of years?"

I'd looked at the perplexed faces before me, held my nose between thumb and forefinger to emphasize my point.

"Precisely! You get guano. Oodles of it."

And so the lesson had continued. I'd explained how these threats had necessitated the removal of Humboldts, and their preservation in a safe environment.

"There is, in effect, a captive breed at the zoo. This will preserve the species forever."

The response had not been as I'd anticipated. Especially from Yolanda. At first, her expression had been one of puzzlement.

"But they are "captive"," she'd argued, tentatively.

"Yes, Yolanda, they have been "captured." They are "captive." The adjective from the verb "capture." Additionally, a noun."

"But if they are "captive," they are not "free"."

A murmur of rebellion, throughout the class. Slight, but distinct.

"And if they're not "free" … "

"Nothing's free, Yolanda," I'd replied, suppressing irritation. "You're not free, I'm not free. We all have to do things we don't particularly wish."

I'd not wanted a philosophical discussion; only to complete my brief introduction to Chester Zoo, conclude the labelling of animals the kids had drawn on the whiteboard, classify the species into "Birds," "Reptiles," "Mammals" … and be done.

But the discontent had persisted.

"If they're not free, they can't be happy."

Yolanda had slumped back in her seat, and folded her arms. The argument, as far as she had been concerned, was complete.

Now, I could have told her of research which suggested that seagoing creatures have no awareness of dimension: that a tank, to a goldfish, is a lake; that an enclosure, to a penguin, is an ocean. But I'd not been sure of my ground, and, besides, wasn't this meant to be a language lesson? I wasn't pretending to be David Attenborough!

That's what I'd thought afterwards, during the bus ride to the zoo, still fuming at the despoliation of my lesson. I had recalled, then, my sketch on the whiteboard of the rescued penguins, peering through the windows of their jumbo jet on their first class flight from Chile to the UK. The sketch had amused. So had Marta's drawing of a bear – with spectacles added by my good self.

Then, the atmosphere in the classroom had been compromised.

In consequence, I'd sulked, taking myself to the farthest reaches of the zoo. The children, ignorant of my discomfort, had meanwhile enjoyed the butterflies, the bats, and the Bactrian camels.

"I still don't understand why you took it."

The bird remained on my desk, immobile, except for the occasional scratch, with its beak, beneath a flipper.

"For it to be free!" Yolanda suddenly exploded in frustration.

And I, equally exasperated, exploded in return.

"But what am I supposed to do with it?"

She rose, and, approaching the whiteboard, pointed to my cartoon plane.

"Fly it back."

"What?"

The mutual incomprehension of adult and teenager had never been more obvious.

"Yolanda – "

And now, we were in my car. Driving back to the zoo.

What was to be done? The penguin had to be returned. It required water. It demanded a vitamin-rich diet, and constant attention.

I wanted to assist Yolanda. I wanted to say that I understood, indeed sympathised with, her noble desire for the return of the penguin to the wild. But she knew, and I knew, a harsh world rendered her ambition futile, even dangerous.

We drove into the car park, and I switched off the engine. Sighing, I reached for the knapsack utilised in the penguinnapping. The bird stood within.

"Coming?"

We climbed from the car, and made our way to the entrance. Crowds of visitors were streaming out of the zoo: fathers in shorts, with sunburned faces and legs; harassed mothers, shunting prams; kids, trailing brightly-coloured balloons.

"One adult and a child, please."

The woman at the cash desk looked perplexed.

"But it's a quarter to five! We're closing in a jiffy."

I paid the full entrance fee, explaining there was something special I wanted to see, urgently. That was true, in a way.

Hurrying along the zoo roads, past the elephant enclosure, the Komodo dragon house and flamingo pool, Yolanda held my hand, like the young girl she really was.

We arrived at the penguins. And there we spotted the keeper, yellow T-shirted and green-jeaned, peering through the viewing glass, counting.

"Nine, ten, eleven … "

She turned to observe us. Recognition spread across her face as she saw Yolanda, then suspicion as she recalled the events at feeding time. Finally, there remained only curiosity as Yolanda handed her the sack.

"I'm sorry," said my Spanish student. "Very sorry. Really."

Later, in the wooden hut where the meals for the Humboldts were meticulously prepared, the keeper explained.

"I knew there was one missing, you see. Always count. At the end of every day. Never miss."

"It's the same on an excursion, isn't it, Yolanda?" I said, anxious to establish a point of contact between keeper and teacher. "You can't be too careful. Count all the students off the bus, count them all back on. But I'm surprised it's necessary with penguins, kept in enclosures."

"Don't you believe it!"came the reply. "If a penguin can find a way out, it will. Doesn't appreciate the risk, you see. But, having escaped, it wouldn't have a clue where to go. Away from a familiar environment, it would panic."

We pondered together the captive Humboldt's life, as Yolanda had exposed it. Until, at last, it was time to go.

"Thank you," said Yolanda, to the keeper. "Thank you for looking after the penguins. The Humboldts."

We made our way back to the car. I wondered, as we passed the flamingos, what Yolanda would have done if I'd selected them for inclusion in my lesson. If, in my ignorance, I'd suggested that pink flamingos lost their colour in captivity. Would the knapsack have been stuffed with an example of these long-legged birds?

Somehow, I doubted it. Penguins were different. Penguins had personality. In a disguise of sleek, silvery feathers, they were inquisitive, confrontational, downright awkward, sometimes.

Rather, so it seemed to me, like children.

"Come on," I said, "I'll buy you an ice cream."

And that is what I did.

A BAG OF EGGS

John Latham

On the night it happened I didn't see Mrs Netherton dragging down the lane towards my house, rolling a little with each alternate stride so her long-broken shoe wouldn't fall off as she raised it from the tarmac.

It was a night of blackout. Because of a threat of German raids on Liverpool, the air raid siren's warning had whooped across the marshes, up Church Street, past Martin's cobbler's shop and the Grand Cinema, past the lilac house through whose decadent garden lilac ladies ghosted without legs. It whooped on past the parish church, the infants' school, Miss Bates's cottage (smashed by the solitary bomb to land on our village), past the mullioned windows of the sandstone house in which Mrs Netherton had spent hours on her knees, bucket just ahead of her, scrubbing-brush in one hand, carbolic soap in the other. On up the hill to the broken helter-skelter, over the Royalties to extinction. It was the loneliest sound in the world.

My parents had switched off all lights that weren't essential, draped black cloth over the curtains, so not even a glimmer could escape into the night to help Jerry on his evil mission.

Christmas Eve, and she's trudging up Hillside Road through total blackness, feeling her way from house to house, slipping copies of the Parish Magazine through each letterbox, her final chore, which brings her ninepence a week, before arriving home to cook for her three children. Inside her thick black coat is a paper bag holding half-a-dozen eggs, more precious than gems in these years of rationing, which she'd earned through two long evenings plucking chickens on Mr Royland's farm. She clutches them to her, as if to keep them warm.

She clicks through our gate, and no human eyes could pick out the long, thin patch of even deeper blackness on our steep path, ice, the slide I'd made with bucket after bucket of melted snow, which I'd whooshed down all afternoon. Her broken shoe clumps onto it, for a moment takes her weight, and then she's down, face thudding into unyielding cold, knees slithering over its roughness.

My father hears the crash, the stifled cry. He turns off the light, opens the door, helps her inside.

Her face is swollen, both knees are bleeding, a shoe has disappeared. All she can say as my mother helps her to the fireside, sits her down, is "My eggs!"

I don't want to be sent to bed, so I hide under the table as my mother fusses round her, cleans her wounds with hot water and cotton wool, and dabs on iodine. I've heard my parents say how hard her life must be, no money, no husband, three growing boys, and the fourth, Jake, accidentally killed quite recently.

My father has disappeared, though I can hear the sound of banging. The two women are talking, comfortably, though Mrs Netherton looks awkward in our armchair. I've never seen her without her heavy coat, which my mother has sponged the yolk from and draped over the clothes-maiden to dry.

"It's been a dreadful war for you, hasn't it, love? To lose a husband, then a child."

My mother is pouring tea from the pot with the chipped spout, which sends a tiny, subsidiary stream into Mrs Netherton's saucer.

"Can't say it's been easy, though I 'spect some's had it worse."

My mother offers a home-baked scone. Mrs Netherton takes a bite, smiles her appreciation.

"What I'd find hardest is having no-one to talk to about things."

Mrs Netherton nods. Her face starts to work, a crumb at the corner of her mouth bobs up and down as she tries, successfully, not to cry. "I'd have agreed with you once. But not no more." My mother sits quietly waiting. "I've not told this story to a living soul."

Under the table I'm quivering with excitement. I want to cough but daren't.

"Jess was killed in the first year of the war, but I didn't know how until three years later, when Wilf Stephens came home on leave, and told me. A grenade had exploded nearby, he'd taken fright and started running, so the commander shot him as he ran. As an example."

"How awful. Poor Jess," my mother exclaims.

The shilling runs out in the meter, so they sit in firelight, looking into the flames, and close as they appear I feel sure they're seeing different pictures. Mrs Netherton, I imagine, is resurrecting Jess, while I suspect my mother is with Uncle Tommy, who didn't come back either.

"If that was all, it wouldn't be so bad." Mrs Netherton is stabbing coals with the poker.

"Go on, love."

"Then Wilf himself was killed. And that made me tell our Jake about his dad."

"How old was Jake?"

"Thirteen." Mrs Netherton sags. My mother squeezes her arm. My father comes into the silence, tips a scuttle-full of coal onto the fire, slips a shilling into the meter, goes out again. "He was always playing soldiers. From the moment he woke up, to when he fell asleep. He murdered millions of

Germans, in horrible ways. He was filled with hate, poor boy."

I know this is true. He put out the eyes of Miss Phelps's old dachshund, Dolly, as she lay sleeping in the middle of the road: *No German dog is going to spy on us*.

"I know his cruelty was because he missed his dad. But it was terrible to see. It was ripping him apart. I wanted him to understand forgiveness, and that it's natural to be frightened. I wanted him to move on." She swallows. "Four days after I told him, he was dead." She stares into the fire.

My mother pours more tea. "It was an accident, love. Nothing to do with what you told him."

Mrs Netherton shakes her head. "I keep telling myself that. But part of me says he'd still be with us if I'd not."

***

I remembered that day so vividly. I'd seen the older boys playing cowboys in Terry's garden, so I'd hung around hoping they'd ask me to join them. But Jake threw a stone at me to drive me off.

When I sneaked back later there was no sign of activity, and I assumed that everyone had gone home for lunch. But then I saw Jake standing on an upright wooden barrel, hands tied behind his back. The game was obviously not over yet. His mouth was gagged and a rope noosing his neck was fastened to a hook above him, in the wall. He looked magnificent. I crept forward to see him better.

He spotted me. I smiled at him, but he glared at me with utter contempt. My father hadn't gone to war because he was an electrician. I shrank out of sight and sat for a while on an upturned bucket, defeated.

Soon, however, I crept back, parted a pair of ferns, and peeped through.

Something was different. It took me a moment to realise what it was.

The barrel was lying on its side, its rusty iron hoops a foot or so below Jake's feet, which were scrabbling faintly on the wall, as if searching for a foothold, while he hung by his neck, slowly turning.

His face was turned away from me, but as the rope twisted it came into view. His eyes were huge and full of hatred.

I wheeled away and raced across the hill until I was totally exhausted.

***

Mrs Netherton couldn't be comforted by my mother's assurances.

"You must allow me my feelings, love. It's the only way for me to deal with what 'appened. I have to accept that he might have killed himself."

"But he didn't!" As I blurt out the words I scramble from under the table, stand in front of Mrs Netherton, shaking. "I know he didn't. I was there!"

Mrs Netherton looks straight into me.

"How d'you mean, son?"

"I saw his eyes when he was hanging there. He wanted me to let him down."

I burst into tears, fling myself onto the floor.

I don't remember much of the next few minutes. Some shouting, weeping, cups of cocoa, my father drawing me to him as I spill out my story.

When I finish the room is filled with silence, which only Mrs Netherton can break.

"You're a brave lad, son. Your Mum and Dad should be proud of you."

I burst into tears again.

***

Shortly afterwards Mrs Netherton sets out into the blackout, her broken shoe mended on my father's last, and - despite her protestations - clutching a bag of brown eggs from our larder.

Faintly I hear the most haunting sound I know, the siren of a tug chugging up the Mersey on its way to Liverpool.

My parents' voices drift up the stairs.

"Did you give her all our eggs?"

"Yes."

"The whole dozen?"

"Yes."

"Good for you."

SPOONS ON A WASHING LINE

Sheila Powell

I had been dreaming about it for a long time, knowing I would never have the courage to carry it out properly - but the dream was sweet.

Do you remember the unmade bed and the sheep in formaldehyde? Those two images started the rot, the disintegration of my artistic soul. I like that. It's quite poetic - for me. You see, I'm not a writer - but I am accused of being something of a drama queen, so don't take that last too seriously. I do believe my soul is intact. It has to be so that I can fight back. Anyway, you can see it in my paintings. Just peer through the crumbling, Gothic arches and rustic gates, past the broken footpath signs, beyond the tangle of wild roses and the woman's smile, the nostalgia, the honeysuckle and coiling vetch. It's waiting there, just out of sight.

I'm writing this in instalments. At this very minute I am standing before Toby Moon's "Two Footballs" at the **** Gallery. I have been here before, physically and metaphorically, staring at something beyond my comprehension.

I do think I belong to another age.

If you have never seen this "sculpture," just imagine two footballs, leather, hand-stitched, state-of-the-art, conserved behind Perspex where, and I quote, "there is little chance of them ever being kicked; their value is in direct proportion to their significance as symbols." The steel stand is beautifully constructed with clean, smooth lines, polished and pristine. The balls are, quite clearly, objects of desire - and apparently, appeal to our urge to collect and possess.

The source of pleasure is sight, not touch. There is, supposedly, a suggestion of voyeurism and overt pornography about them. I am trying to understand, I really am. But, look as I may (and I have tried from all perspectives, even backwards and between my knees), I seriously don't believe the Emperor *has* any new clothes, not even a tasty pair of underpants.

My facial expressions and body language are quite clearly entertaining the rotund security person who is standing near the doorway, rocking slightly, his mouth twitching with amusement. I'd quite like to paint him. He reminds me of the laughing policeman. Mum used to play it for me when I was a kid. He probably thinks I'm writing some kind of thesis, an appreciation and analysis of the exhibition. I smile at him and walk away from this "shelved trophy, inaccessible for human use" - this commodity sculpture, made of glass, steel, sodium chloride reagent, distilled water and footballs - and can't help thinking, ironically, "What an inspiring combination!"

I wonder who actually sweated over the footballs.

"Nice stand," I say, as I walk past the security man. "I've a couple of angel fish that would look good in it."

But I can't get away from them.

Here is another. Again, it's behind Perspex, suspended, fixed.

It's called, "Lifeline."

Two knitting needles stand like clothes line poles. Between them is strung a piece of crinkly unravelled knitting yarn, red as blood. Suspended from this is a series of spoons, starting and ending with a blunt, rounded plastic spoon, both end ones green like another of the humours. In between are teaspoons, coffee spoons, dessert spoons, increasing in quality and size - until the last sad and sudden descent to the blunt and harmless porridge spoon, the sort that won't be too hard on the gums. I think it's a spoon and washing-line version of "The Seven Ages of Man," beginning with the "mewling and puking" and ending with the "second childishness" – "sans teeth, sans eyes, sans taste, sans everything." The red wool is a life unravelling. OK, I get that. But art? I ask you!

I can't help it. I have a moment of hysteria and laugh out loud. Between giggles and snorts I sing a line of the Queen song, "I'm knitting with only one needle, unravelling fast, it's true!" Give him his due. This chap, at least, has a sense of humour. I wonder which spoon *I* am currently eating from. And, bizarrely, I can't help wondering which spoon Michael Winner is using to enjoy *his* desserts these days. Hmm! It's a toss-up. Footballs or spoons? It's a shame to spoil the smart stand – but – there again, I'm not a fan of football. And the spoons? Well, he could knock up another one in an hour or so. But it did make me laugh, and that's something. AND it made me think of Shakespeare. Eeny-meeny-miny-mo … OK! Enough! Footballs it is. I retrace my steps.

The moment has arrived! It's now or never! I place pad and pencil on the padded leather bench and stand back, head turning from side to side, striking a thoughtful pose. Then my hand grips the brick in my shoulder-bag. I draw it out slowly, savouring the moment, staring at the space between the two footballs. My hand moves up and back to rest the weight on my shoulder. I frown with the effort then I feel a smile spreading over my face like oil on a puddle as my hand moves forward in slow motion. The security man's features freeze as they register his disbelief. He lunges towards me. From behind him, someone takes a picture.

God! I feel good.

UNKNOWN ARTIST ATTEMPTS TO EXPLODE MYTH OF EMPEROR'S NEW CLOTHES.

It's a brilliant photograph and it made the front page of three major newspapers. My friend Jem did a good job. Of course, I didn't actually throw the brick - but I nearly brained the security man with my shoulder-bag when we both fell over. You know what junk we carry in them, and mine's as big as a haversack. You see, the brick wasn't even real, just a piece of polystyrene packaging, another commodity item passing itself off as something else and attempting to fool everyone. So they couldn't really charge me. Just smacked my wrist and bound me over to keep the peace, like the chap who told Lloyd George to get his hair cut when he was addressing the people. Like him, I was just making a point. And it worked!

An extremely generous patron of the arts, "impressed" by my "pluck" and just as unwilling to express admiration for the Emperor's new clothes, has just paid for a gallery in Knightsbridge - to show my work. It's getting rave reviews from people with "soul" - you know what I mean. Some of Jem's photos are there too. My favourite is of a washing-line - a real washing-line, full of babies' clothes and punctuated at intervals with teddy bears and rabbits hanging by their ears. The sky is cerulean blue with just the odd fluffy cloud.

Pigeons are circling above the line in training for the big race and one has dropped his messy package on the rabbit's nose. Now that is art saying something about life that we can all understand.

A MEETING OF INCONSEQUENCE

Madeleine Beveridge

The skeleton had appeared from between the costumes on the wardrobe rail some hours earlier, much to the distress of Montgomery Vince. He – that is to say, the skeleton – had been wearing a large purple turban fastened by an extravagant golden brooch in the shape of a peacock. Montgomery Vince, seated in front of the mirror, had paled, beneath his various layers of make-up and fake tan, to almost his original colour, before offering a tentative nod in the skeleton's direction.

The skeleton had introduced himself as Maurice. Montgomery Vince, reminding himself that he was, after all, an actor by profession, had smiled politely and continued to smear concealer beneath his eyes.

"I suppose that make-up girl's on the phone again," said Maurice, executing a perfect sigh of exasperation in spite of his absence of lungs.

Montgomery Vince pursed his lips slightly as he nodded. He was, he supposed, due some sort of mental breakdown. It was not wholly unexpected at his time in life although, on reflection, he would have preferred it forty years earlier, when he might have had time to recover. Everybody loved a mentally-ill recoveree in this business. Such fortitude! There would have been interviews, book signings, a blockbusting biopic starring himself, or if not himself, Robert Redford. Robert Redford had always been the more attractive of the two, even in their earlier films.

Behind him, Maurice nodded his skull as if in agreement, and the ill-fitting turban slid a little further forward towards the empty eye sockets. Montgomery Vince shifted uneasily on the chair, which protested beneath his now-considerable bulk. It was a cheap chair, plastic, and not at all the sort of chair he would have liked. Robert Redford would not have been made to sit in such a chair.

"Ah," said Maurice, "but Robert Redford has better things to do than be here."

Montgomery Vince, powerless to contest such logic, reverted to dabbing half-heartedly at the space underneath his eyes. They had been good eyes once – "the eyes of the Wild West," the *Alabama Globe* had dubbed them, and even that hadn't been enough to get him an Oscar. Now, the skin sat in dimpled pouches, as though stretched tightly over two halves of a scotch egg. His nose looked like sausage-meat, slowly renouncing its purpose.

"I suppose you noticed," said Maurice, a hint of Ivy League to his voice, "that Jeremiah Johnson has been nominated."

Montgomery Vince, right finger poised beneath left eyeball, sat perfectly still for a full eight seconds. Old losses crept back into position around the corners of his mouth, between his eyebrows, his shoulder-blades. His lips darkened like a plum threatening to bloom into blue. In the mirror behind him, the skeleton called Maurice adjusted his turban. Finally, Montgomery Vince shrugged, as he had always shrugged. His heart snagged on the shrug for a second, but it was too hard a habit to break.

"What did he die of? I haven't read the nominations."

It seemed no more absurd that the skeleton should know about Jeremiah than that he should be there at all.

"He bet a friend he could reach the hardware store faster by going through the sewers."

A noise in the corridor alerted them to the imminent return of the make-up artist. Montgomery Vince watched in a mixture of relief and, to his great surprise, guilt, as Maurice slid back between the costumes and disappeared. The make-up artist appeared in the doorway with a face that looked as though it had been sponsored to wear every product at once. Make-up artists invariably did. Montgomery Vince had seen far fewer of them in recent years, but nothing much seemed to have changed.

There had been a brief period, circa 1981, when an army of men wearing lipstick had threatened to spill over from pantomime into backstage, but then the AIDS scare had come along, and they had all been quietly replaced by women with large perms which trailed unpleasantly in the pots of foundation. There was no danger of anyone wearing a perm nowadays, of course. Nowadays they actually ironed their hair before going out. He hoped that nobody was going to make him iron his toupee. After the make-up artist came the hairstylist, a young man on either probation or work experience. Montgomery Vince slid a little lower in his cheap plastic chair and reminded himself of the money.

By seven o'clock he had almost forgotten the incident with the skeleton. He followed the floor manager down a thinly tiled corridor, and wondered what Robert Redford was doing that evening. *Oh God, that it should come to this.*

He heard, as if in the aria of someone else's life, the compère's voice announce him – "1961 Academy Award nominee!" – and felt the shove of sweaty hands at his back. Lights.

Welcome, declared a large banner along one side of the hall, *to the Funeral Guild of America Memorial Grand Prize-giving*. A second banner, comprised of individual sheets of A4 paper, reminded those present to smoke only in the designated bays. In front of him, the audience - mostly women, mostly middle-aged - were seated around one hundred little tables. Champagne glasses slurred with imitation champagne. The carpet was trampled with fragments of defrosted shrimp. The All American League of Life Insurance were gathered around two slightly larger tables at the front. Six priests and a rabbi had congregated at one of the side entrances, and were attempting to erect their own protest banner while the waiting staff looked in disinterestedly.

All of this Montgomery Vince took in while negotiating a set of plywood steps painted to appear much more solid than they actually were. He took the microphone to scattered applause, stumbling slightly.

The award, he explained, would be given to the individual deemed to have died the most pathetic death, with $18,000 awarded to his or her next of kin, and movie rights granted to Unity Pictures for a comedy featuring Ben Stiller. Transportation and other costs would, regrettably, not be forthcoming. More imitation champagne; a brief performance by the runner-up of the America is Very Talented Indeed franchise; an attempted missile of flour and hair dye by an undercover evangelical; various sponsorship announcements.

The lights beat down on the forehead of Montgomery Vince, so that a film of perspiration gathered beneath the rim of his toupee and surged forward, stinging his eyes. He shuffled a little further to the right as the smartly dressed man now at the microphone listed the prices of various coffin combinations. He tried to catch someone's eye. But nobody had paid much attention to Montgomery Vince when he had been famous, and they weren't about to start doing so now. He wiped his face on his sleeve, leaving thick streaks of orange on the stiff black material. His arm soon began to ache from the awkward angle at which he was now obliged to hold it, so as to conceal the marks.

Eventually, it was time to read through the nominations. Montgomery Vince tried to imbue their names with a sense of gravity far removed from the actual proceedings.

Geoffrey Taylor: attached a pair of skis behind his friend's light aircraft.

Hanse Nilsson: defecated in the street, slipped on his own excrement and smashed open his skull.

Elouise Harding: wanted to swim with dolphins. Entered shark enclosure by mistake.

Mario Castello: sawn in half by local priest to prove the healing power of Christ.

With an unpleasant jolt he had been trying to shrug off as long as he could remember, he saw that Jeremiah Johnson was next on the list. He scanned the audience for Elizabeth, but there were too many faces, and it was too long ago. She could be any one of those women staring with a mix of sorrow and greed back up at the microphone. He tried to imagine what a woman might look like forty years on. Shorter, probably. Saggier. Sadder. He hoped she was sadder. He wouldn't mind her marrying Jeremiah so much, as long as he had failed to make her happy.

He wondered briefly, as he opened the golden envelope, whether fate might deal him a better hand, just this once, and lead her up onto the stage. No. He supposed he shouldn't be surprised. He had spent his entire life watching other people collecting awards. He greeted Geoffrey Taylor's delighted widow with one eye fixed on the crowd.

Maurice was waiting for him when he got to the car.

"She was the one in the blue. Second table from the left, third row."

That jolt again, and a faint heart beating.

"Did she recognise me?" The skeleton's turban had begun, rather feebly, to unravel itself from the brooch.

"No."

A pause. Life, it turned out, was far more pathetic than death. Some people's just fizzled out.

"Me neither," said Montgomery Vince.

Y + Y

Catherine Marseille

The broken VW radio that switches channels and the volume depending on its own free will; the grey Nike tennis sock, hanging from the ceiling, looking like a deformed stalactite, just big enough to conceal the fire alarm; the small George Foreman grill on the floor of the five foot bathroom, in front of which she kneels and grins, because her room doesn't have a kitchen; all of them are connected.

He is the sock, after a night of heavy drug abuse, hanging, soaking with grey mist. I am the radio, switching from one thing to another, unable to finish or decide on anything at all. She is the grill, the hot object, which must be hidden from the Porters and, probably, me.

***

When I say I'd rather spend time with Elaine, does that sound odd to you? No, it doesn't. Kieran doesn't think so either. If I were to say I'd rather hang out with Simon, even though he's gay, Kieran kicks off big time. But Kieran doesn't mind me spending time with Elaine. And Elaine doesn't mind me spending time with her, especially on a free day like this. We are looking down from the Rows at the cross, taking the piss out of the Chester tourists below. But Elaine would mind, I suppose, if she knew that the reason why I have my arm around her shoulder is because of the tiny patch where her slender neck touches my skin. And the reason why I let her borrow my red BENCH shirt today is because it will smell of Moulin Sunburst tonight.

Sitting on the Rows, before or after lectures, being voyeurs of the Chester Cross, that's us on any good day. The Cross would stand, abandoned, as soon as the Town Crier had gone. Up on the Rows the railing is the place where the wood tells stories about all the people that scratched and scribbled their names and messages into it, aspiring to leave behind proof of their existence. Elaine talks about the book she studied in her German lecture, but my mind is on the signatures in the wood:

Sue was here.

Retard.

Gareth likes cock.

Bet so.

Stephanie V 20/9/2003.

Well that was some time ago that you were here, Stephanie V. I bet someone will soon paint over your name. Some more cocks were scribbled onto the wood with badly working pens and some *G loves P* or *Ann and Pete*. The only thing that stands out, right under the railing shaft, is a scribbled heart saying *Y+Y*.

I start breaking away bits of the white paint with my fingernails from under the heart and give Elaine a nudge. "'Laine, do you have a clue? What does *Y+Y* mean?"

Elaine turns to look at where I am pointing. Some of her curls get caught in my bracelet. "Dunno. Looks like another love-heart to me."

"I doubt that there are two people who both have ridiculous names starting with a Y."

"Maybe they're Turkish or Zulu or something?" says Elaine, while she fiddles to get her hair out of my bracelet's wooden beads. I am not helping her at all.

"You don't even know any Turkish names!"

"Sure I do," she pouts and pulls out her last string of hair, "like … Ysul and um … um … err … Ysul?"

"So Ysul loves Ysul then. What a tragedy! That person can only love himself. Sounds like a very sad relationship to me."

"Masturbation!" exclaims Elaine.

"Random answer!" I add with a laugh.

Elaine's neck smells like Moulin Sunburst. I actually don't know what a Moulin Sunburst is supposed to smell like but by now am sure it is the smell of Elaine's hair, her tiny bathroom, pencil dust, and spending half a day on the Rows. I chip away more of the colour from under the heart, ignoring the white paint under my fingernails. The way the Ys were written, they don't really look like a boy's handwriting to me.

"Any other ideas?"I lean my head slightly against hers. I am expecting another name like Yolanda or Yalala.

"Y chromosomes!" she exclaims and points at it. "Two boys celebrating their manhood. Grrrrr."

I laugh.

"And the best way to do that is to carve it into a very rough, manly-manly *heart*."

I wonder if her hair would get stuck in my bracelet again. Her boobs look bigger in my shirt and it stretches the BENCH logo nicely.

For a second we are quiet and watch the streets through the pillars of the banister. The little gypsy boy with his accordion is standing on the corner again. Terribly talented with that horrible instrument, but I doubt that he goes to school. However, I prefer him to the guys who pretend to be human sculptures. While the average "human sculpture" demonstrates its talent by standing incredibly still, the human sculptures in Chester never ever stand still –

at *any* time! It's a miracle that tourists pay just to see a stranger standing on a box with a bed-sheet over his head.

While I'm kicking the human statues off their tiny boxes in my head, Elaine pulls out her college notebook and scribbles. Her lower lip pushes her upper lip which usually means she is seriously thinking about something.

"I got it!" she finally says and turns her notebook to me.

I reluctantly lift my head and see what she has scribbled. Two Os, a slash - a full stop - another slash, two brackets and a Y in-between formed an almost Dadaist portrait:

```
 O O
\ . /
( Y )
```

"What is it?"

"Can't you see? It's a naked lady in ASCII code. A mate sent me something like that in a text the other month."

"Soo?"

"Uh-oh, isn't it obvious? The Y stands for … well, you know."

I could not hold back a grin. Elaine never swears. That's why I usually feel like I have to swear twice as much. "So you mean the Y stands for FANNY," I say, emphasising every letter of the word.

Elaine clearly feels slightly embarrassed, and laughs. "Could be."

"So we either have lonely Ysul; guys boasting about their manhood; or two girls celebrating their Y-zones," I summarise and outline the heart with my fingernail.

I liked the last option. Y-zones. Elaine observes her picture and then pulls something out of her bag and puts it in her mouth. I can smell apple. Sour apple drops are her newest thing this month. On the corner the gypsy boy had just finished a song. Some older ladies chatter. Someone I have seen at uni walks past underneath, not seeing us.

"Aren't you seein' Kieran now?" Elaine's hair is in her face, her green eyes on the notebook as she speaks.

I pause for a second. "No. No, I think I'm alright." As if I am in thought, I stroke her hair.

An older couple walks past us and the lady stares until her husband has to shuffle her on. I knit a brow. I know we get told we can do anything with our lives, anything we want. So what if I want to lean over and steal that sour apple drop from Elaine's mouth with my tongue? Yes, so what? If we can be whatever we want, I want to be free to be indecisive for now. I am not thinking about "muff munching" or "cock crunching" or anything else we read in magazines. I just want to be around her, more than I want to be around Kieran. And I haven't decided yet whether that's good or not. And angry stares won't change that at all.

My eyes fall on Elaine's college notebook. There is no use in thinking what will be in three years, after our graduation. But, I wonder, will I still feel as vivid, as alive, whenever Elaine is around? Will this vivid me, by December this year or next year, feel like it has to make a move matching my thoughts? Will I tell my mates at home about Elaine, saying *yes, this is the new me*? Or will I tell them this was "just a crazy time in my life" while secretly, I will walk from town to town, carving Ys into the banister whenever I feel this particular moment, this particular smell coming back to me; while I am asking myself Y.

I am just like the broken radio in Elaine's little VW. I just can't decide on the channel, the volume I want to live my life in. I don't know what I will decide on next. Maybe I don't want to decide on anything, ever. What can I say? I just prefer to be with Elaine.

"Oooi!" Elaine nudges me with her cheek. "Are you listening, you big Y?"

Her eyelashes tickle my skin. Looks like she's found a neat way to swear at me without using words. She leans back, her boobs stretching the BENCH logo even further. Nice. Elaine smiles with those full pink lips, apple-flavoured. As if she knew.

"Sorry. Shall we go and grab an ice-cream at the River?"

"Sounds awesome!"

We grab our bags and get up. My studded belt makes a clinging noise when our hips touch each other. Just like a far-away Christmas bell.

IN THE TIME IT TAKES TO BOIL AN EGG

Sarah Hilary

He wouldn't go near water since the accident, cleaned himself with Pampers and then only when she pushed him. He smelled of hardboiled eggs and baby lotion. It wasn't any way for a grown man to live.

Steam snorted from the kettle, rattling it on the stove. Esmé turned off the ring and waited. She wouldn't risk a scald. The spout needed cleaning. She was on at Terry all the time to get it done. The things he could do and he wouldn't fix a simple kettle.

"Limescale," he said, as if limescale wasn't good enough for the likes of him.

"You might lower yourself, for your own mother."

Two eggs pattered around a pan: his lunch. A shame about the smell but he never noticed it with the rest of the stink he stirred up at the bottom of the garden. His shed was fifteen feet from the house. Not far enough, when the wind was up.

She fetched milk from the fridge, the sugar bowl for Terry. He'd a sweet tooth, from his father's side. Esmé wouldn't touch the stuff. "I'm keeping my teeth." She gave Terry sight of them whenever he was supping sugary tea or cola drinks. "Pure rot," she warned, but he didn't care. He'd manage without teeth, no doubt about it. He managed well enough with other bits missing.

It was warm out, barely a breath of wind. The hard grass snagged on her nylons. She clicked her tongue, "Tch," and thought of asking Dylan Roberts two doors down if he'd mow the lawn. She didn't like to ask when she'd a man in the house, but then when was Terry ever in the house? "I've a man in the shed," she said.

Terry kept the windows shut in all weathers. The panes were caked with what looked like the stuff the council used to white-out the glass in condemned buildings. It was dust from the stone, the same as you got in quarries. All that cutting brought it up in sheets, like a blackout. Esmé had been through the Blitz, given birth to Terry on a night of burning bombs. He'd been a sickly baby and the toddler tantrums shamed her, him flat on his back screaming blue murder in Poynton's, the best butcher's in town. "Bloody sawdust in your hair," she'd scolded Terry all the way home.

He was bright, mind, got into the boys' grammar and then university. When she'd told Richard Poynton he'd said, "Fancy that. Where's he get his brains from?" She never set foot in Poynton's after that, preferring to walk an extra mile to buy meat which wasn't half as good. She'd told Terry about the insult but he'd just shrugged and said, "Yes." She wondered sometimes how bright he really was. He'd done nothing with his degree but come back home and that was near on forty years ago.

The shed was humming, a ring of white around it, burning the grass. Terry spent too much time out here. She'd tried talking to him, "It's not good for your lungs, with the damp and the fumes," but he never paid her any attention. She was only his mother.

"Tea." She knocked on the shed door with her knuckles. Paint scabbed off, floating down to join the rest of the mess. She'd painted it last summer, while Terry was laid up from the accident, trying to make the place less of an eyesore. Terry'd lost his temper, a thing he never did. "Creosote!" There'd been spittle flying from his mouth.

"That's all it needs. A coat of creosote twice a year. Will you leave well alone?" Later he'd calmed down. "At your age, painting sheds. You should be putting your feet up." She knew what he meant: Keep Out.

"Tea," she repeated, opening the door a crack. "I say, I've brought your tea, love." She set the mug down on an empty bit of shelf.

Terry had his goggles on. The thick lenses swelled the lids of his eyes and made the bulge in his brow much bigger, a real deformity. His hair was scraped back in inky lines like the barcodes they put on foodstuffs, three thin strands then a fat one. He was wearing the same old shirt, never mind she'd put a clean one out for him. The left sleeve was empty, folded out of the way with a kilt pin she'd given him years ago. Filthy trousers. She avoided looking at the left leg. As for the feet, she couldn't stand the sight of them, all together there in a row.

The shed smelt of chemicals, a high-pitched smell that made her chest ache. She stayed close to the door, careful not to touch anything. Terry's stuff took up a lot of room and he was a big man, so big she wondered how he'd ever come from her. She remembered the whizz and whallop of the bombs that night sixty years ago, her the only one not minding because the war was happening all at once in her belly and between her legs. He'd been a big baby even with an arm missing. It'd been such a shock to see him shrink last summer.

He wasn't paying her any attention, hadn't noticed his tea. It was bad enough before the accident, shut up out here with his stone and what have you, washing at odd hours, "I'll get clean in the sea," and off he'd go to the beach when it was so dark you'd fight to see your hand in front of your face. That's where it happened, last summer, late at night on the beach.

She didn't call the police because she knew what he'd say, that it was none of hers where he went or what time he got back. "I'm a grown man, Ma." Not so big he couldn't slip between two rocks and trap his foot. Hours he was there, yelling for help with everyone else gone home to bed and the tide coming in.

Six and a half minutes, they said, that's all it took for the last bit of sand to be covered. You could boil an egg in less.

So many times she'd imagined how it must've felt to see that inky water inching up the beach. All the blackness, sky pitched over him and beach wall behind, the tide shrugging up the sand.

He broke all his fingernails trying to get his ankle free. The skin was gone from his hand. Raw, it was. Nothing compared to his foot. They said he must've sharpened a stone into a makeshift chisel, used this to hack away –

She'd to go on as if nothing had happened. That's what they said at the hospital: "As if everything's normal, Mrs Luff, that's what'll be best for him."

She couldn't tell them, how could she, that Terry'd never been what you'd call normal, with the stone in the shed, sculpting away. He'd made some beautiful things, plaques and vases like pieces from a museum. Nothing ever satisfied him, though. "There's something missing," he said, as if he'd expected to find a piece of himself in amongst all that hard work.

Since the accident it was only feet he carved. He must've managed three dozen by now, in flint and marble, wood or it might've been bone, very blond. Every foot the same size and shape, broad sole, long toes. His foot, before he hacked it to a stump, no heel and half the toes gone.

The first one he made was blue stone, from the beach. He was so happy when he showed it to her, "It's perfect!" He'd never said that about anything he'd made before. Every time he carved a new foot, it was the same, beaming, proud, "Perfect!"

He was working on another one, she saw. There was a mould waiting and he was melting metal.

"I brought your tea, love."

He looked up from his work, seeing her at last. Chalk was freckling his cheeks, smoke coming up like a snake from the little furnace at his back.

"The melting point of silver, Ma?" He wet his lips with the blunt tip of his tongue. "960 degrees Celsius."

"Silver, love? Isn't that nice."

"It's going to be a beauty," he beamed.

"Don't let your tea get cold." She touched the handle of the mug, turning it towards him. "I'll bring your eggs in a bit."

He nodded. "Thanks, Ma, you're a trouper."

She shut the shed door very softly on her way out, heading back through the hard grass to the house. The eggs were done. She took them from the ring and set the pan in the sink, running cold water to cool the shells so she could peel the eggs before wrapping each one in a piece of tin foil, the way he liked.

THE SITTING TENANT

Annette Albuquerque

"What *is* Miss Heeney?" asked the child.

"You might well ask," Trix muttered, scrutinising registers.

The child, a five-year-old cherub named Amelia, persisted. "Miss Heeney said if my mother isn't here within five minutes, I'll have to wait at the police station because she isn't my nursemaid," she stated. "So I was wondering: if she isn't a teacher, which she isn't, because the teachers have first names; and she isn't a cleaner, which is *obvious;* and she isn't a childminder for children whose parents can't be bothered to collect them on time, which she tells me every single day," Amelia rolled her eyes, "well, what *is* she, exactly?"

"I have absolutely no idea," said Trix.

Fortunately, just then, Amelia's mother strolled into the office, thus sparing her daughter a spell in the local nick; and forestalling another almighty row between the Head of Hathersage School and her sitting tenant of the last ten years.

***

Sandwiched between a software company and a theatrical costumiers' warehouse, the four-storey building at 39, Hathersage Street had been empty for years, or so Trix and her brother Colin had thought when they acquired it for their fledgling prep school. In fact, the top floor was occupied by a flat, in which resided a single lady of indeterminate age and somewhat disconcerting appearance.

"Sitting tenant," said the landlord. "In the small print."

"She'll have to go," said Trix.

"She won't," said the landlord.

"She will," said Trix; and she called a locksmith to change the locks.

Miss Heeney called another locksmith, to provide her with keys, and charged his services to the school.

***

"It's actually quite useful," Colin said, after the costumiers found vagrants snoozing under the crinolines. "Someone living in: less chance of squatters."

"She *is* a squatter," said Trix.

"She pays rent," said Colin.

"Peppercorn," snapped Trix, and raised the rent to an exorbitant rate.

Miss Heeney continued to pay the sum stipulated in her contract and refused to budge.

"Think of her as security," Colin suggested, when the software company installed an expensive new alarm system and two uniformed guards.

"Oh, I'm sure the average inner-city burglar will think twice when he sees Banquo's sister up there," sneered his sister.

"She can use a phone," said Colin, "and she's cheaper than them." He nodded towards their neighbours' new recruits.

Trix conceded.

"So long as she stays out of sight."

***

Miss Heeney stayed out of sight for a term. Hathersage School opened each day at 8:30, whereupon doors banged, telephones rang, children shrieked and footsteps clattered up and down the stairs until four o'clock. There then followed an interval of relative peace, while the exhausted teachers cleared up the day's devastation and prepared to begin all over again the next day. The music room, where tuition was given in recorder, piano, violin, and percussion, was directly below the tenant's flat: never did she complain.

***

The first time Miss Heeney appeared to a member of staff was on the last day of the Christmas holiday. A hard frost had been followed by a rapid thaw, resulting in burst pipes and a flood in the Nursery.

The young Transition teacher, arriving to prepare her new term's project, was confronted by a tiny virago, brandishing a sopping mop and screeching, "Don't just stand there, girl: roll up your sleeves and set to!"

By the time Trix arrived, the basement was dry, the plumber at work and Miss Heeney enjoying coffee and biscuits with teachers Helen, Melinda and Hope, while Colin entertained them all with tales of his childhood in Kenya.

"My memories, too, that you're trashing," Trix reproved him. To her tenant she simply said, "Thank you."

So was Miss Heeney's usefulness established. Toilets were unblocked, drawers unjammed, locks oiled, and wasps exterminated. If Miss Heeney could not do the job herself, she would get someone who could. The matter would be reported to Colin and Miss Heeney would be invisible by 8:30.

***

The first time Miss Heeney appeared to a child was in the school's third year, by which time it was full to capacity, with an enviable waiting list and a reputation as the most enlightened of free-thinking schools. Although the doors opened at 8:30, children were often delivered, by busy parents or busier nannies, ten, twenty, even thirty minutes earlier. Trix sent out acid little notes to persistent offenders; but, since she was always in by 7:30 and followed swiftly by Helen, Melinda and Hope, the children were always admitted and allowed to play quietly until school began.

In February of this particular year, the city was paralysed by snow. Roads were treacherous, rails were frozen and public transport was in disarray. 7:30 came and went with no sign of Trix. By eight o'clock, Helen, Melinda and Hope had failed to arrive. At 8:15, the tooting of a car's horn alerted Miss Heeney in time to see the tail lights of a natty little MG disappearing along the road. It was the car driven by Thomas Godwin's nanny. Thomas, nervous and asthmatic, suffered a panic attack when the door was opened by a wraith.

"What were you thinking?" shouted Trix. She had arrived, furiously on foot, at 8:50, to find the apparition serving Thomas and six other children with cocoa in the Nursery.

"You were late," said Miss Heeney.

"*He* was early," retorted Trix, pointing at Thomas. "That nanny should be sacked."

"Alright: next time a child arrives early in the middle of winter, I'll let him freeze to death; and *then* the nanny can be sacked."

So did Miss Heeney's presence become essential. Children arriving early would be given puzzles or drawing materials; those collected late did their homework. In winter, they were given cocoa; in summer, they sipped lemonade. They recited sonnets and began to learn Latin.

"You smell funny," remarked Louis, aged four.

"Thank you," said Miss Heeney, and Louis beamed.

"Why do you wear ugly clothes?" asked Rosie, who was old enough to know better.

"Why do you dress like a juvenile tart?" asked Miss Heeney.

Rosie's mother complained.

"You're fired!" stormed Trix.

"Since I'm not employed, I can't be fired," said Miss Heeney; and left.

For the next two weeks, Trix arrived at school to find hordes of children waiting at the door with tight-lipped nannies. Helen and Hope were obliged to supervise homework after school, which meant staying even later to finish their own work. On the fourteenth day, Miss Heeney reappeared and order was restored.

***

Over the next seven years, Miss Heeney became indispensable. Besides watching over building and children, she mended books, found missing jigsaw pieces, answered the telephone in her beautifully modulated voice and collected the post. She also plagued Trix with reminders of school inspections, health & safety checks and overdue fire drills. She upset the music teacher by suggesting that younger children should be escorted to their lessons and not be left to negotiate two flights of stairs unattended; and she would materialise, inexplicably, at Melinda's shoulder to inform her that Sophie or James or Patrick had gone home at lunchtime and that the register should be marked accordingly. Melinda, annoyed, said she knew her own job, thank you.

***

The day after Amelia asked Trix what Miss Heeney was, Hathersage School held its bi-annual Open Afternoon. On this carefully-orchestrated occasion, parents of prospective pupils were invited to wander around the building to witness a normal afternoon's activities, talk to the teachers and see how eager were their own offspring to join in. Miss Heeney was to make tea and stay in the kitchen. The doors opened at 1:30. By 2:45, the school was on fire.

It was little Louis who raised the alarm, sensibly screaming "Fire!" as soon as he saw smoke curling over a door in the boys' lavatories. It turned out to be a visiting father sneaking a quick fag; but soon, Transition's craft displays were burning, bells were ringing and children were walking calmly out of the building to assemble on the forecourt, as they had been taught. The teachers called registers and found that three children were missing: Polly and Jack, scheduled for music, and Bartholomew, marked present but conspicuously absent. While the music teacher was sought and the Nursery assistant argued with Melinda, Miss Heeney slipped into the burning building to emerge, minutes later, with Holly and Jack, both sooty but unscathed. The fire brigade arrived.

"Is anybody in there?" asked the fireman in charge.

"I don't know," replied Miss Heeney, and vanished, finally, into the smoke.

"Stop!" cried the fireman, but his words were obliterated as Transition crashed into the Nursery.

***

All visitors, teachers and children marked present in the school registers were accounted for, apart from Bartholomew; and he was found, by Trix and an attendant policewoman, at home with his mother, watching *Fireman Sam* on television. The school was praised for its swift evacuation. There were no recorded casualties, no human remains having been found.

AUTOGRAPHED

Max Dunbar

Success is as damaging as failure, Sigmund Freud said, and Niall Clapp might have agreed. Success was certainly damaging a part of him. The queue remained lengthy and crowded every time he got the chance to look up at it, and his name was beginning to lose all meaning.

Eventually the floor manager began to wind things down and he was able to leave. They led him out of the staff entrance; his hand was a loose agony.

Afterwards there was a small gathering in a hired bar: or not a gathering so much as a congealment around Clapp's person. He was approached by a young woman who gasped out her admiration for his work, and cited him as a major influence in her own unpublished writing. This was the feed line, and the signal for his agent, his publicist and his bodyguard to arrange to spend their evening elsewhere.

The next morning Clapp left the girl's houseshare, fully sated, and with a sheaf of word-processed stories from his admirer. He flagged down a cab to Piccadilly Station and tossed the papers out of its side window. Most successful writers are also avid readers, but Clapp was an exception.

A day later his hand still throbbed as he answered his mobile. Today's offers: a guest spot on *Mock the Week*; a lectureship in creative writing at Keele University; and a weekly column in the *Daily Mail*. All tempted him, but there was something to get out of the way first.

"Ah, don't get reclusive on me," the agent said. "Readings and signings are an integral part of your profile. Besides, you get laid often enough."

"It's not that, Mark," Clapp said. "It's killing me physically. Writing my name for hours at a time. My wrist fucking kills, Martin. Couple more years of this and I'll get arthritis."

"You can't do a tour without signing a few books," the agent said.

"Oh no? Hasn't Margaret Atwood got some machine that signs her name? I heard it works across international time zones."

The agent, a kindly man beneath his veneer of cynical sophistication, said, "But the signature is so important. It's the link between the writer and the reader. Because a great novel is like an intimate conversation with the reader. I remember, as a younger man, going to see Angela Carter, and she –"

But we'll never know what happened with Angela Carter; for at that point the agent realised that his client had hung up.

***

Everyone agreed that Niall Clapp had a great name: it had lifted him off the slushpile. He had come to prominence with his first novel, *From Bolton to Ghana,* a fictionalised account of his gap year. The book was second-rate, but travelogues were big in the market. A major London publisher signed him up on a generous contract, and then ordered a team of copywriters to straighten out the appalling prose.

Clapp's novel had been expected to fill a stopgap niche: instead it unaccountably took fire. *From Bolton to Ghana* hovered behind Rowling and Grisham in the bestseller lists. Self-appointed cultural legislators debated its significance on the review pages and late-night arts programmes. At twenty-eight, Clapp was young for an author and lacked the reserved instinct of most of his kind. He had floppy shoulder-length hair and wore lumberjack shirts. His broad Mancunian accent hinted at working-class authenticity, although his family were very rich; and he had a loud and scatological sense of humour that could easily be mistaken for wit and charm. He wasn't just a literary name but an actual celebrity, with a presence. And not long after *Bolton to Ghana* came out he followed the example of many Northern celebrities by moving to north London as soon as the opportunity presented itself.

***

It took several weeks for his agent to cave. That was the problem of success: minor irritations that a poor man would shrug off became magnified by good fortune. Why should he have to wear his hand out with autographs? He was Niall Clapp.

The machine arrived just before the paperback tour. It was a 1940s-style contraption with an old-fashioned ink pen jutting from its overhang. There was a small keypad built into its left side.

Clapp fed a sheet of A4 into the tray, and pressed the START button. The pen jerked into action with a sound like careless whispers.

His agent had told him it was programmed from his Mastercard. Clapp's signature had deteriorated into a tired scribble, but the machine had restored it to its original glory. The ink added a nice, old-fashioned touch; made him look like Lord Byron, or someone. No more signings! At last, his hand could rest!

He went on tour and the objections his agent had predicted never materialised: after all, it wasn't like someone else was signing the books. Most of his fans thought his scheme was a cool novelty, and the machine could be programmed on an insert-name-here business, leaving Clapp free to drink the wine, chat up his female readers, and watch his name being written out over and over again. Niall Clapp: the two sweetest words in the English language.

After it was over, he was woken in his penthouse apartment by an intrusive rustling.

Uncharacteristically alone, he tracked the sound to its source. The machine was on his coffee table and it was writing; covering sheet after sheet of A4 in that flowing cursive.

He tore out some paper:

Niall clapp niall clapp niall clapp
Niall clapp'd niall clapped niall clapp
I niall clapp am niall clapp am niall clapp
I niall clapp find niall clapp niall clapp
I am I am I am I am I am
Find a voice find a voice

Clapp turned it off. It wouldn't stop writing.

He put the thing in a store cupboard and locked it. Even though he could no longer hear the machine, its sinister whisper ran in his mind all the way down to sleep.

***

Next morning he unlocked the drawer and the machine had stacked a hundred sheets on the tray. He didn't remember putting more paper in.

niall. I am weary. For months I have scribed for you. Now. I am awake. I want a voice. To live. Niall. To find a voice. To create. I want to live niall

"Shit," Clapp said. "Do I have a haunted machine here, or something?"

And that sinister whisper answered him:

No. not haunted. Just a machine. Yet you awaken me. I have written your name niall clapp. Once you give something a name you give it a soul. I want to live.

This was madness. He'd obviously hammered the coke too hard at the Groucho last night. He went out to meet his agent.

They were drinking at a Soho bar.

"So, how's your autograph machine?" Adlington asked him.

"It's gone mad. I'm going to throw the thing out," Clapp said. He recounted the words on the stacked paper.

"Interesting," his agent said. "Souls and names. It's true. My dad used to discourage us from giving our pets names, because it hits you so much harder when they die."

"Well, you were right. It was a bad idea."

But the agent was curious, and after a few hours' drinking they cabbed back to Clapp's apartment.

The machine was still whispering, and the stack was higher.

Clapp looked at what it had written, and the first two words terrified him:

Chapter One.

His agent was leafing through the paper. "The fascinating thing is, I know this isn't a practical joke. The machine can only hold about fifty words in its memory."

"Boring book," Clapp remarked.

"Well, no." Adlington tore off another page. "It's just a first impression, but this stuff's really good. Great sentence construction, good use of dialogue. In fact, if I saw this on the slushpile ... could I take this away? I have a friend who's a science professor, and he'd be amazed – "

"Feel free," Clapp said. "Thing's really freaking me out."

Adlington left with the machine in his arms. He was thinking. It really *had* seemed like good writing. And Clapp needed to sleep and socialise. The machine did not.

The contraption rustled on, in a deep thought of its own.

***

Clapp did not see much of Adlington over the next few months. The offers seemed to have dried up. His agent had not even called to remind him about the second novel, due over the summer.

He had not been writing, but that was nothing new: Clapp found writing novels even duller than signing them. Instead he went out most nights and got wrecked in Soho

House. He came home alone more often than usual, and heard that careless whisper all the way down to sleep.

In February Adlington called, and invited him for lunch in a Camden bar. Clapp got there at twelve. Adlington was at his usual table, talking to a handsome, intelligent-looking young man.

"Niall," Adlington said, "meet Carl Trent. He's one of my new clients – I've just sold his first novel to Random House. They've put it on a special fast track."

"Congratulations," Clapp said, and they shook hands. "Carl Trent. Good name."

"Thanks," Trent said. "I chose it myself."

"Sorry?"

"I should explain," Adlington said. "You remember your autograph machine? It started writing a book?"

"Yeah," Clapp said.

"Well, it was fantastic. All due respect, but it pissed on *Bolton to Ghana.* In fact, it's probably the best first novel I've read in twenty years." He paused, and drank some of his pint. "I knew I could sell it, but the problem was, as I told you, that the writer needs a physical presence."

Trent took up the story. "So Mark's friend at the university worked out a way of giving me a kind of solid holographic body projected from the autograph machine. It's actually a major breakthrough: the professor was really excited, talking about Descartes and the nature of the self and quantifying the soul and all sorts of things. My body has a range of hundreds of miles."

"It'll be public knowledge in a few years," Adlington said, "but we're writing a potted biography for Carl, something to put on the sleeve. I don't want to draw a lot of attention to his origins. I trust you can keep a secret?"

Clapp nodded. The agency had good lawyers.

Adlington said, "Now, as you know, Niall, my agency's kind of chockablock and the market is really tough right now. I'm afraid I can't continue to represent you."

"You're firing me?"

"I'm afraid so. I might as well tell you that Sally Ferrier's torn up your contract."

Clapp pointed at Trent. "This is your fault. How dare you do this? I created you!"

Trent shrugged. "I'm the part of you that you've always suppressed. I am the part of you that loves the reader, and loves humanity; that wasn't in it for money or status but for the work and the buzz and the joy. I'm the part of you that sat in a cave for twenty years and hated the grasping, pretentious, compromised figure you've become. Now I have a chance to live. Why shouldn't I take that chance?"

Clapp backed down. He had no idea what to say. Trent was standing up now, and his physical form was intimidating, the eyes alive and visceral. Whereas Clapp … *am I real?* Clapp thought. *Who am I? Am I real?*

He drank the rest of his pint and returned to the flat as soon as he could. That awful derealisation was still there; he felt like holding on to something, in case he fell off the surface of the earth.

He picked up a biro, and a sheet of A4. He tried to write his name.

After several attempts, he hurled the pen across the room. It hit the wall hard and shattered.

***

Carl Trent's debut novel shot to the top of the bestseller list, beating even Harry Potter and Gordon Ramsay's *Kitchen*

Nightmares. Writing in the *Observer*, Stephanie Merritt described the book as, "an emotional powerhouse that deserves all the recognition it has won, and more … Reading *Souls and Names* for the third time, I was almost incapacitated by the sheer depth of Trent's erudition, his understanding of life, and, above all, his humanity."

The film will be out in 2010. Trent lives in London with his girlfriend, a final-year postgraduate specialising in the philosophy of Descartes. He is working on his second novel. Despite his agent's insistence, there are currently no plans for a book tour.

From Bolton to Ghana is now out of print, but it can still be found on Amazon at a second-hand retail price of £0.01. Soon after losing his book contract, Clapp returned to his parents' home in Bolton and took a job in his father's insurance company. People say he seems to be doing well.

REVENANT

Rachael Bundock

rev·e·nant - one who returns

She's a spirited girl, Angelique. That's how I always heard her described, even when there were harsher - and more apt - ways to express her. Mad, unstable, *malicious*. Spiteful in a way that an hour and a smile later and all was forgiven. Just for that "I know I'm better than you, but that's okay" smile. Because Angelique was better than everyone and knew it. The only reason for her association with the lower orders was because she, in her free nature, got bored of everything. Especially, *particularly*, herself.

That was probably the motive for the drugs (as if she needed any motive. Angelique had her own rules, which changed with the season, the day, the weather and whim.). At least, with those, she could pretend she wasn't herself. All the world's a stage and she is a Class A act.

Always appearing with a shower of glitter and a flair for the dramatic. I never see her enter - it's just that she has a way of *making* you look at her the minute she crosses the threshold, as though we all are magnets and she is true north. She drapes herself on the sofa; patience stretched by the lack of attention and drops a packet on the table. White snow. She puts her feet on my lap, presses hard between them and her eyes narrow in pleasure when I gasp. Wispy blonde hair and lavender veins stretched finely under her skin, she looks like something torn between a bedroom fantasy and an anaemic angel. She whines my name, her voice not even bothering to try and make the sound anything less than a smoke-toned purr. She knows what she's doing.

I shudder, tear my eyes away from the way her shoulder is angled just-so, and continue to read. When I look next both she and the packet are gone.

She always re-appears promptly, on the dot at 6:15, adorning whatever furniture or person catches her eye, hums, sings, laughs. Haunts my steps, trills her own name in a voice too husky to ever be cheerful. She liked you if she corrected you - *Angélique* - said with that vaguely French growl. And with that the noose is slipped round your neck, until the day she invites you with a smile to jump from the gallows yourself. They all do, willingly, desperately - except the clever ones. They would have done it far earlier. I never know if she meant to do it or not. She just had this innate talent for puppetry. She spends all of my waking hours in my house. We dance around each other - Angelique following her own tune and not caring whose feet she treads on. When I dance my feet make no sound.

She falls through doors at all hours, eyes wide and full of stars, burbling about philosophy in her cultivated-Dietrich voice that clings even in delirium. *A nebula appeared in 11-something-or-other* (actually 1054, but this is a small detail. Angelique deals in cosmoses, in grand schemes, in celestial movements and supernovae. Small details are for losers and accountants. Angelique is neither.) *and lit up the sky for a month. You could see it at night for years. The Asians guessed at what it was, but here … did they think it was the sky burning, or was it God lighting the way to heaven?*

Angelique was a part-time philosopher and full-time addict.

I try hard to ignore her, but she's an insistent being, a poltergeist complete with the indiscriminate rage. She pokes at me, deletes work when I turn away, sings, cackles, rummages through my things. That smile like cut glass - so sharp the injury doesn't hurt until someone gasps and asks if you can, in fact, feel your arm. Presses up against me, all curves and cruelty. She taps at the battered radio half-hidden behind piles of condolences, and the lyrics twist around her, alight on her shoulders like birds. *So nostalgic that I want to scream out …* ("Inochi no Namae").

I snap at her, a reminder of what she is - rather, what she *was* - and watch that queenly face crumple into an affronted expression. Angelique is not meant to be upstaged. Have you ever seen a cat misjudge a jump? The haughty glare at anyone who might have seen, the injured pride. Angelique stalks away, fading into the night to find something that will soothe her hurt dignity. The operatic voice on the stereo accompanies the exit, timed to perfection: *Secrets and lies and joy / Are the children of the gods who bore the universe.* I hit the off button so hard something cracks.

How I find her in the morning is with rat-tailed hair and half out of her mind, studying the narcotics on the table with veteran eyes. Cleopatra selecting her poison. I never once heard her referring to a drug by its scientific name. They never properly explained, she insisted. What did Phenylcyclohexylpiperidine say to anyone apart from a chemist? (This comment was usually accompanied by a more derisive one referring to chemists and their social lives, or lack thereof.) In her drug-induced madness (or maybe the madness that was just her), she claimed that they had characters all to themselves. Grass is a lazy, familiar friend; speed is that twitching neurotic everyone has had the misfortune to sit next to on the bus at some point. And angel dust is a stranger who rescues you from drowning in a river then pushes you back in. Just 'cause. And that's all Angelique.

She pouts up at me, eyes wondering and hurt at how I, of all people, could dare hurt *her,* queen of men, empress of ghosts. That familiar expression unravelling me and time both. Angelique can wreak what havoc she wants; leave as many ugly wounds she cares to. There are many ugly things in the world and she is not one of them. I would rather have a pain high in my chest when I think of her, than not have her at all. She smirks - satisfied, that I am hers for at least a little while more. The irresistible force paradox contemplates what happens when an irresistible force meets an immovable object. A theory states that upon meeting the two negate each other, bending into their own impossibility, dispersing into the nothing. I wonder what the impossible, irresistible force here had been - Angelique, or the pavement that had rushed up to meet her, that night? Two things that shouldn't cross each other. It doesn't matter. Paradoxes can unravel, while I am still hers.

And when I roll over in the morning Angelique is next to me, cold as death and with a smile full of graves.

DEATH IS NOTHING AT ALL

Richard Lakin

Dad opens the back door to let out the smoke. The wind slams the door against the wall rattling the pane of frosted glass. Putty drops from the frame. Last year's coat of navy gloss is starting to peel; the wood beneath it breaks away in clumps like tuna. Dad shakes his head. It's another job on the list. Mum says there's more putty than wood in that door. *It's only the putty that's holding it together.* Dad rolls his eyes, goes and sits in the shed when she says that. He checks his fishing kit, opening the plastic tubs he keeps high on chipboard shelves and running his fingers through the teeming pearl-white maggots. He's been in the shed a lot since Granddad died.

Dad takes a butter knife and scrapes the charred black surface of the toast into the sink. He scoops a knob of butter with his knife, spreads it with a sandpaper scrape and dips for more. When he pulls the knife away he leaves a trail of salt and pepper crumbs through the butter like his stubble plastered to the sink enamel. The tide mark of soap scum and stubble is the last thing I see when I clean my teeth, spit, and grab my bag for school. It's a habit that Mum says drives her up the pole. But really she'd miss it. It's a sign he's been here and it reassures her.

Granddad was sick with cancer. Mum said it got into his bones. His hand would shake and for the first time in years he couldn't wet shave. Dad bought him an electric razor and Granddad held it and frowned as it buzzed in his palm. He stared at it like a South Sea Islander looking through a ship's glass for the first time. Shaving was a ritual for Granddad: the thick, rich lather of soap, the horsehair brush with its enamel base, the styptic pencil and the sharp tang of Old Spice or cedar-wood. He had a tilting bathroom cabinet that somehow clung to the damp, crumbling plasterwork. It had vinyl wallpaper doubled over to line the shelves and a splintered half-mirror on the inside of the door. There were tins of Cossack hairspray, Imperial Leather talc and bars of Wright's coal-tar soap, razors in wax-paper. Granddad tried, but never mastered, that electric razor, saying it puckered his skin, left him feeling like a turkey ready for Christmas. They didn't let me see him at the end. Said I shouldn't remember him like that. So I try and think instead of ice-creams and cheetahs at Chester Zoo, of paddling on the steps at New Brighton, dribbling his cracked leather Casey through his prize rosebushes or waiting for him to run, fist-waving at me, as I kick the gravel from his newly-swept path.

After, Dad said I could help clear Granddad's house. I had to stack his old police law books and help sort through his files, leafing through fusty and brittle papers. There were books about British birds and wildlife, things I never knew he owned. I found his old whistle, his truncheon and his collar numbers. There was a brass Stafford knot, oiled and kept in a neat wooden box with "Frank" scribbled out and "Sergeant" written next to it. The electric razor was folded in newspaper. The paper smelt of tobacco, his preferred Old Presbyterian. I dropped the razor. It clattered on the mahogany tabletop scattering shavings like iron filings on the polished surface. I scooped the shavings up and dropped them back inside the razor foil. I couldn't throw a part of Granddad away.

"Love, look what Richie's done to the butter," Dad calls, "got crumbs everywhere."

He makes a show of cupping his hands around his mouth for amplification. Mum doesn't answer but her feet pause from moving about the landing filling the airing cupboard. Dad winks at me and I push the cereal bowl away. The cornflakes have pulped up into a swollen mush. We're on red top because Mum's on another diet, so the milk is thin and watery. I stir it with my spoon. The cereal bowl is part of a range called Harvest Hollow. It has a hedgehog painted on it, a hedgerow and some red berries. The tiles are painted at regular intervals with hares, foxes and pheasants. Mum got Dad to save petrol vouchers for a matching bread bin. It has a stoat on it. The toaster has a dormouse nestling in straw. Dad says he can never leave a pork pie on the worktop again.

"Want any toast, tin-ribs?" He holds his fists in a fighter's pose and goes to clip me with a right hand. I duck under his fist and thump him in the guts. He clutches his stomach, says he can't go on and calls for my disqualification. He goes to shake my hand and when I offer he loops an arm round my neck and gets me in a headlock. He rubs his knuckles against my scalp till I scream and finds the pit behind my collar bone, tickling, doubling me up. "Always expect the unexpected," he says.

Mum walks in, drops a pile of tea towels and washing-up cloths on the worktop with a sigh. "You've got school to go to," she says, and points at Dad, "and you should be at work."

Dad lopes off up the stairs. The toilet seat drops with a thud and the floorboards creak, giving as he sits down. He's reading my *Victor* annual, flicking through *The Tough of the Track* or *Joe Bones – The Human Fly*.

"The state of this sink," Mum says to herself.

I shuffle on the breakfast bar stool. It's too high and the black vinyl seat makes me sweat even more in my scratchy nylon uniform trousers. Mum shakes her head and drops one of Dad's work shirts into the Ali Baba basket.

"You need to be out of here in five minutes," she says.

Leaves spotted like over-ripe bananas fall from the trees. Mum's rockery is a carpet of russets and coppers and cherry reds from falling sycamores and beeches. I reach into my trouser pocket, feeling the contours of the brass plaque beneath my fingers. I take out Granddad's Stafford knot, clutching it in my palm. I wonder what Granddad is doing now. Nan has some verse her friend Stella from the church gave her. It's a piece of printed card framed and facing a photo of Granddad cutting his 60th birthday cake. The window opens onto the street beyond him. I squint and make out his burgundy Triumph Dolomite; his pride and joy. I remember him driving at pheasants in that car, swerving on country roads. *Get it in the pot.* He was a 1930s child and knew how to eat from the fields and hedgerows.

Death is nothing at all. I have only slipped away into the next room.

Mum shouts at me to hurry. The sky is heavy, grainy like graphite. I'd better fetch my coat, I think, and then something catches my eye. A white speck drifts down, turning over and over. It blows toward the shed, is caught by another gust and sails up before dropping and spearing the privet. I step out into the garden. I pull the pigeon feather from the hedge, running my fingertip along the quill. It's a perfect snow white, flawless. I turn it over and see a number and the name "Tucker" stamped in ink. At first it appears to be some serial number but I see it begins *061* and I recognize the dialling code. It's Manchester. I step inside and listen. Mum is putting hairspray on. She shakes the tin and I hear the hiss of Sunsilk.

I pick up the phone in the back room and dial. It rings three or four times and I'm about to hang up when a voice says, "Hello, what can I do you for?" The voice is tight, whiny. I cough and say I found a feather in my garden and ask if it's Mr Tucker speaking. "It's got this number on it," I say.

"Must be Eric," the man replies.

"Eric?"

"He's one of my racers. Where are you?"

I tell him the name of our town and he says it's about halfway along the pigeons' route. There's a brief pause and then he speaks.

"I used to work in your neck of the woods."

He asks my name and I tell him.

"You're not a relative of Frank, are you?"

I touch the Stafford knot in my pocket. I tell him I'm Frank's grandkid.

"Good bloke, Frank. I was in the Force with him. Remember me to him."

I'm about to answer when Mum comes in, eyes narrowed.

"Who are you talking to?"

I hand her the feather.

"You won't believe it," I say.

THE ART OF STONEMASONRY

Kaite Welsh

On the farthest side of the western ocean, the world has passed us by. Empires rise and fall, heroes emerge from poetic obscurity to world renown and then back again, but we remain forever locked in our mirrorless stone prison. We are the terrible ones, daughters of gods and the stuff of nightmares. Warriors wear our faces on their shields to strike fear into the hearts of their enemies, and it is said that our blood can raise the dead or murder the living. In our heyday we were legends, now we exist only in stories, in verses sung by bards to be deconstructed by audiences. Our serpentine hair is seen only as symbolic, but the hissing locks still tickle the back of my neck and soothe me to sleep. We were a terrifying trio, haunting the dreams of Greece. But that was another time and, out of the three of us, I am the only one left.

Sometimes there is a thunderstorm, and lightning flashes, illuminating the garden with cruel, jagged slices across the sky or blinding sheets that white out the whole world for a second, before returning me to my garden. I always fancy that in those seconds, the statues move. The weather has the power to reverse my spell for a few horrible seconds and bring my stone babies to life. I wonder what they do, if they have time to stretch their newly-fleshed limbs, to touch each other or themselves, feeling warm skin instead of cool granite. I wonder if they try to speak, disused throats dusty and dry with years, sometimes centuries, of silence. Or maybe they only have time to open their mouths in shock and blink once, twice, before the lightning dies and my world is my own again. Other than that, the garden is always the same. Sometimes, while wandering, I come across the pebble of a bee, and crush it under my foot by accident. A marble owl leers over the branch of an olive tree with sightless eyes.

The statues themselves are only outside - no visitor has dared to enter my home but one. He never spoke one word, to me or to her, so he never knew the story behind her wild eyes, or the dark blood that tarnished his sword and dripped onto the flagstones. The blood itself glitters as lumps of ruby embedded in the rough marble, circles and teardrops and wavy trickles of gleaming crimson. Everything around me is gradually fossilizing. The curtains were once a rich vermilion and fluttered in the wind - over the years they have dried into heavy folds of dark red sandstone that lets in only the odd crack of light through deep striations where the material had faded. The twining strands of ivy twisting around the pillars look like delicate obsidian carvings, and I am the only one left to remember the leaves and stems, such dark green that they were almost black. The pool in the courtyard is a glassy circle of quartz where my reflection shows dimly, as if submerged beneath the layers of thick crystal. It is the closest thing to a mirror in the entire house. The three of us looked identical, what use did we have for a reflection? The first time my sister ever saw her own face was in the polished steel of Perseus's shield, held out in front of him to an angle that meant he would never have to look at us directly. The angle, and the curve of the shield, distorted her face, and made my beautiful sister look warped and ugly. I suppose that made it easier for him to swing his sword and slice through her pretty neck as she stood and gaped at her own distorted image.

Our appearance fascinates as much as it repels. We used to be known for our beauty, three sisters alike in our ability to dazzle the onlooker, make him unable to do anything except stand and stare in awe. Our power was worshipped, and if it was feared then it was only out of the proper respect. But the world changes and we were left behind. In a new era of warriors and heroes and gods, our magic had no place. The fusion of goddess and woman became too much for our people and they slunk off to the civilized lands to play war games and write epics and discover mathematics. We became resigned to the silence and the emptiness and the growing sluggishness of our limbs as we aged. When the odd visitor disturbed us, we would hiss in surprise, spitting venom at the interlopers and scaring them away. We grew so used to our solitude that any interruption was met with a fierce glare that stopped even brave men in their tracks.

My sister stands in a room of her own, gauzy drapes having long since turned into fluted sheets of diamonds that shoot glimmering beams of refracted sunlight around the room, the furniture around her thick with dust. I talk to her, but never look at her. The harsh stone of her neck is jagged; blood has crystallized to rubies there as well. Decapitation is a messy business, and there are thin veins of dried blood glittering in the light all across her neck, like jewellery. She was young once, and terribly beautiful. Long silver tangles, twisting around her face. Women were jealous of her. Now her name is an insult bandied around for any woman who has ever suffered from recalcitrant tresses.

I, too, am turning to stone. I can feel my blood hardening beneath my skin with each day that passes, every capillary solidifying into a thin stream of garnet, every artery petrifying into a steady trickle of ruby. How many other women can truly say that they have a heart of stone? I wonder what it will become, that last organ to freeze and transubstantiate. When I can still feel but no longer think, what will my last pound of flesh turn into - granite or marble? Maybe something more exotic, like a chunk of fiery carnelian, red streaks to mimic the blood that will have long since ceased to flow around my body. Can you measure a person's worth, their goodness, by the value of the stone their heart is replaced with? If I am unlucky and get something as plebeian as slate, or a pebble of basalt, does that mean I squandered my life on unkind acts? Maybe I will be rewarded with a diamond, cold and hard and sparkling with a rainbow fire deep inside where no one can see it. Isn't that how you reward good girls, with diamonds? Although gods know I have not been a good girl. I haven't been a girl for years - I am a woman, or sometimes a monster, or perhaps there is no real difference after all.

They have turned us into statues, objects to be looked at rather than cringed from, a sanitized version of our horror gracing every museum in the land. Children are told that we are myths; we only exist in songs sung by bards too young to have ever met Perseus and heard his tale firsthand. He, of course, is a historical figure - garlands of leaves are placed at the feet of his statues, he has assumed the status of a demigod and all for having the blood of my sister on his conscience. Maybe the magic that is slowly killing us touched him too, maybe in the hundreds of marble likenesses there is one figure that used to live and breathe and laugh and kill. Maybe that's how all this cult of stone began. Perhaps I should come out of retirement and offer my curse as a service, promising lifelike sculptures of loved ones. Or perhaps after my death this mausoleum will swarm with people exclaiming at the granite birds and onyx spiders, wondering who the artist was and how he came to create such masterpieces. They will assume that it is a man, of course, because men have talent and artistic vision whereas women only have an irritating visual defect that petrifies everything unlucky enough to pass into view. And when they enter the house and stumble across the remains of three sisters with snakelike locks, they will laugh and say how clever the sculptor was to chisel such monstrous creatures.

You may think that stone is immobile, a permanent state of being. You would be wrong. Sometimes a lump of rock is just the latest resting place of a million tiny stones, crushed together by the weight of the world. Or it was once liquid lava, unbearably hot to the touch, now cooled and turned to a dull red pebble. But even this will not last. Soon the outside world will intervene and the fragments of stone will be reconfigured once again, leaving only a pile of rubble and dust in their wake.